ALVIN CHARLES BAILEY WAS FOURTEEN WHEN HE FIRST SHOT A MAN TO DEATH.

The gun he used was a .44 cap-and-ball Army Colt. The man he killed was a big bearded hulk named Thomas Whisler, who wouldn't pay for the two dozen bundles of maize he'd bought from the Bailey family.

"Pop said I got to get the money," Alvin had said.

"What about I give you a kick in the ass instead?"

Rough hands had grabbed the boy and spun him around. A size twelve boot kicked him in the seat of the pants so hard he fell and skinned his hands on the rocky ground. It was the last thing Thomas Whisler ever did.

At home, Alvin told everyone what he'd done, and the Bailey family spent most of the night praying. The killing had to be reported to the law, but not before the boy had saddled a horse and headed out of eastern New Mexico territory to Mount Capulin, where his dad's brother lived. He carried a loaf of bread, a small iron skillet, and a pound of cured ham. And his prized Army Colt.

At fourteen, Alvin Charles Bailey was a killer and a fugitive. By the time he was twenty, he'd killed a dozen men.

Now he was about to kill again.

DOYLE TRENT
NIGHT
RIDER

ZEBRA BOOKS
KENSINGTON PUBLISHING CORP.

ZEBRA BOOKS

are published by

Kensington Publishing Corp.
475 Park Avenue South
New York, NY 10016

First printing: March, 1992

Printed in the United States of America

One

He crossed the Rio Grande twice, hoping to throw them off his trail. Just south of Pilar, where the river poured out of a deep gorge, he crossed again. The bay horse was up to its belly in swift water, pushing through the cottonwoods and winding around the black malpais. The man was carrying a Colt double action .38 in a low-cut holster on his right hip. A pair of saddlebags and a thin blanket roll rode behind the cantle of his saddle. His plan was to follow the gorge into the Taos Mountains, where he would cross the river for the last time and get on the west side of the deep split that divided northern New Mexico Territory right down the middle.

Traveling would have been easier on the wagon road, but he didn't want to be seen. Keeping the gorge on his left, he came out of the lava hills onto a wide sagebrush prairie that stretched for miles in three directions. Flat as a table. He urged the weary horse into a steady trot, hoping to reach the foot of the mountains before dark. The gorge was invisible now, but he knew it was there, hidden in the sagebrush, deep and steep. A man and horse could fall into it if they didn't watch where they were going. By the time he saw Taos, the sun was a couple of hours from the top of the Conejos ridges. Small white clouds drifted under the sun, causing dark spots of shadows on the mountain slopes.

His name was Bailey. Alvin Charles Bailey, also known as A.C., better known as Ace.

Ace Bailey. Wanted. Dead or alive.

Still paralleling the gorge, he kept the village of Taos far to the east, with only a few flat-topped adobe shacks visible above the sagebrush.

At the tiny settlement of Arroyo Hondo he had to make a decision. It sat near the edge of the split, and he could either ride through it or go wide to the east to get around it without being seen. Hell, he mused silently, if that sheriff and his bunch were still on his trail, they would spend the night in Taos. By the time they picked up his trail in the morning, he would have found a place to cross the river and would be headed back south to Albuquerque. He could stand on the west side of the gorge and make faces at the sheriff.

No, that wouldn't be smart. Not smart at all. The lawmen could get fresh horses at Taos, while his horse would get little feed and rest. If they knew where he was headed, they might catch him.

He called the horse Booger Bay, and the gelding was a good one. But it had been a long, hard ride from Las Vegas. Climbing those mountains would be even harder. Ace Bailey had never ridden a horse down. He'd face an armed mob rather than kill a good horse. He had to find a fresh one.

Instead of going east to get around Arroyo Hondo, he turned the bay to the wagon road and headed right down the one street. Not much of a settlement. A few adobe shacks. One house built of lava rock. A long building, half adobe and half lumber, had a wide porch and a sign over the door that read; "Groceries." The adobe part of the walls was crumbling, and someone had stretched chickenwire across it to hold it together. Only four men were on the street watching him ride by, three of them Mexicans with sandals on their feet and wide straw hats on their heads. The one white man wore a rancher's hat and high-heeled riding boots. He had a walnut-handled pistol in a holster on his left hip, butt forward.

Ace Bailey figured him to be a rancher and no threat, and he ignored the man's stare. Up the street a ways, four horses were tied to a hitchrail in front of another long building, this one of pine logs. The door was wide open. He dismounted there, wrapped the reins once around the hitchrail, and walked in.

The settlement was not a place where travelers were often

6

seen. Taos yes, but not Arroyo Hondo. The half-dozen men gathered at the far end of a long plank counter inside stopped talking and gave him a good looking over. What they saw was a young man, not much older than a kid, with straw-colored hair sticking out from under a wide-brimmed black hat. He was handsome with a day's growth of blond whiskers, a straight nose, a wide mouth, and flat-planed cheeks. Forcing a smile, he stepped up to the bar and said, "Whiskey."

"*Si, senor.*" The fat bartender had a small moustache that needed trimming and wore a dirty white shirt. His black hair grew low on his forehead. He took a bottle from under the bar and poured whiskey into a shot glass. "Twenty-five ceents, *senor.*"

Bailey dug a coin out of his pants pocket and tossed it onto the bar. "*Gracias.*" He sipped the whiskey, then studied the men on the other end of the bar. Two appeared to be cowboys and the others he guessed to be Mexican farmers. "I'm traveling through," he said to them, "and I could use a fresh horse. Know where I can make a trade?"

No one answered.

"I've got a good bay gelding outside that can outrun anything for a couple hundred yards, but he needs rest."

"You lookin' for a hoss race?" The speaker was or had been a cowboy. He was short, with big-roweled spurs on his boots.

Grinning, Bailey drawled, "Naw. Not now. I'm headed for Albukirk, but I don't know this country and I got on the wrong side of that big ditch over there. How far north does that damned arroyo go, anyway?"

"If you're headed for Albukirk, you'd best go back south."

"You're prob'ly right. I thought I could get across it if I kept heading north."

"You can, but you'll have to do some climbin'."

"Well, anyway, my horse needs some rest and good feed, and I ain't got time to kill. I'm ready to talk trading."

"Well," said the cowboy, "let's see what you got to trade,"

Four men, Anglos and a Mexican, followed him out to the hitchrail. He unwrapped the reins and led the horse a few steps. "Sound as a Yankee dollar. Five-year-old. See them

7

muscles on his hindquarters. He can jump into a dead run in two seconds. Ain't a horse in the territory he can't jump ahead of."

The men walked around the gelding, looking him over. The short cowboy pried its mouth open and looked at the teeth. "Comin' seven, I'd say."

"Nope," Bailey argued. "Five-year-old. He just got his full mouth."

"Well." The cowboy ran his hands down the horse's forelegs, feeling for splints. "Let's see 'im move."

Shaking his head, Bailey said, "He's plumb worn out. Otherwise I wouldn't trade him for anything. It would be cruelty to animals to make him run right now."

The cowboy squinted at the Conejos Mountains, at the ground, and at Bailey. "Got a bill of sale?"

"Yep."

"Well, I got a good grey gelding that'd make a fair trade. He's had a good rest since the last time I rode 'im, and he can take you a long ways. Only I got to have some boot."

"Let's see him."

The crowd followed the short cowboy and Ace Bailey across two vacant lots to a two-room badly weathered adobe shack. A lean-to and a corral made of vertical juniper sticks was behind it. A grey gelding stood in the corral, watching them approach.

"That's him. He's a good 'un. Gentle enough to put your kids on if you got any. Eight-year-old. Just right for a travelin' man."

The grey was longer in the back and legs than the bay. Except for the color, it was the kind of horse Bailey wanted. A man on a grey horse was too easy to identify. But he needed the animal.

They dickered. The cowboy asked fifty dollars to boot. Smiling, Bailey talked him down to ten. "No matter how much you pay for my horse, he'll win it back in the first race. But don't race him very far. He's a sprinter, not a runner." The cowboy agreed to throw in a coffeepot, coffee, and four pounds of jerked beef.

Leading the grey, they trooped back to the saloon. There,

Bailey put his saddle on the horse, then went into the saloon, had a shot of whiskey, and wrote a note that read: "I, Alvin Charles Bailey, did on August 1, in the year 1886, trade a bay gelding, unbranded, about fifteen hands, and weighing about 1100 pounds, to one J.W. Swanson at Arroyo Hondo, Territory of New Mexico." It took him four minutes to write the note. J.W. Swanson read it twice, then said, "Bailey? Ain't I heared that name someplace?"

Smiling, Ace said, "Could be. I got relations all over the territory. Except here."

And just as the sun went behind the Conejos hills, Ace Bailey was on his way again, still going north, saying he'd cross the river wherever he could. Fifteen minutes before dark he unsaddled and picketed the horse on a thirty-foot rope. The river arroyo was passable here, but he figured it would be dangerous in the near darkness. On foot, he followed a narrow path down into it and filled the coffeepot, then climbed back on top. His supper was boiled coffee and very tough beef jerky. The more he chewed, the bigger the mouthful got. But that was expected, considering that it took three pounds of beef to make a pound of jerky. While he chewed he pondered his predicament — and made another decision.

He wouldn't go to Albuquerque. He'd told the men at Arroyo Hondo he was going there and they'd tell the sheriff — if the sheriff got that far. No, he'd go on north, get on the wagon road that went up and over the Taos Mountains and down to the town of Cimarron. From there he'd go back home and see how long he could stay before some lawman came nosing around and asking questions. That decided, he wrapped a blanket around himself and lay on the ground, using his hat for a pillow.

Ace Bailey was used to sleeping on the ground and he slept well, but at daylight he found himself in a worse predicament. A lot worse. The horse was gone. The rope had been broken about ten feet from the small boulder it was tied to. Twenty feet from there, the ground had been torn up by horses' hooves. Something had stampeded the horse. Bailey looked for bear tracks and found nothing. No other tracks at all. He'd known horses that panicked when they were left tied

9

alone. They fought the rope and either broke loose or hurt themselves trying. Was this one of them? Reckon so. Why didn't the short cowboy warn him about that? Because he wanted to get rid of the horse, that's why. Dishonest? Not entirely. A horse trader's credo was to tell no lies but not to volunteer negative information, either. Nothing to do now but walk. He had a coffeepot, some coffee and jerky. A Mexican could walk a long way on nothing more than that. But Ace Bailey didn't like walking. He'd walk, but no farther than back to Arroyo Hondo.

Wrapping the coffeepot in the blanket, he shouldered it and walked, leaving his saddle under a tree. At least he was walking downhill. He approached the settlement carefully, keeping low and out of sight. The street was empty. The only human he saw was a Mexican woman feeding some chickens in a wire pen behind a crumbling adobe shack. Still keeping low, he half circled the village until he could see the shack and the corral where the grey horse had been kept. The horse was there, walking around the corral, dragging a broken rope. While Bailey watched, the short cowboy came out of the shack, caught the horse, and put it in the corral with the bay and another horse, a black gelding. Then he fed the animals from a stack of hay in another, smaller pen and went back inside the shack.

Silently, Bailey wondered how many times the cowboy had traded off the grey horse. Out loud, he cursed. "All right, you sonofabitch, you know I'm afoot. You could at least come looking for me." Feeling anger boil up inside, Ace Bailey stood and walked directly to the shack.

He stood just outside the one door and hollered, "Hello." The short cowboy came out, chewing his breakfast. His face showed no surprise at seeing Bailey. He had a cocked hogleg pistol in his hand.

"The trade's off," Bailey said. "I want another horse and my ten dollars back. You didn't tell me the horse won't stand tied."

Shaking his head and swallowing, the man said, "Uh-uh. A swap's a swap." He pointed the pistol at Bailey's middle. "Besides, I figured out who you are. You're Ace Bailey.

You're a wanted man."

"So," Bailey said, standing relaxed, thumbs hooked inside his gunbelt, "you're either gonna shoot me or run me off. Either way, you get my horse and ten dollars for nothing. Maybe you'll even go through my pockets to see what else you can find."

The hog-leg pistol didn't waver. The finger on the trigger was steady. "The easiest way," the man said through tight jaws, "is to put a bullet in you."

A familiar tingle worked its way into Bailey's body. It started in his limbs and creeped into his stomach and chest. He stood relaxed, even smiling a little. But in his mind he knew.

He was going to kill this man.

Two

Alvin Charles Bailey had been fourteen when he first shot a man to death. The gun he used was a .44 cap-and-ball Army Colt. He'd spent a week hoeing weeds out of a neighbor's potato field to earn it, and it was his proudest possession. As long as he could buy the powder and percussion caps, he practiced with it. His dad and older brother Jim showed him how to melt lead and make his own .44 caliber balls. The Baileys farmed eighty acres of floodplain along the North Cimarron River in northeastern New Mexico Territory. They'd migrated west to get away from the carpetbag government and lawmen of East Texas. The law in the Territory of New Mexico wasn't much better, but at least the people had some say in it. The Anglos did, Mexicans didn't vote. The senior Bailey grew vegetables, sweet corn, and maize, and he preached in a one-room rock building on Sunday mornings. He called himself a Baptist, but the denomination didn't matter to the small congregation as long as he preached hell's fire and brimstone.

Maize was the Bailey family's main crop. The stalks and the grain tassels at the top provided livestock with both grain and roughage. The whole family — Papa, Mama, two boys, and a twelve-year-old girl named Mindy — worked at harvesting it. They cut it with scythes, tied it in bundles, and stacked it. Cattlemen were the best customers. They were glad to pay for feed for the horses they kept up in the winter. But two dozen bundles had gone to a man who lived in a clapboard cabin near the Oklahoma border, a big bearded hulk named Thomas Whisler. Alvin and Jim had hauled the bundles over there in a wagon one day, but Mr. Whisler wasn't at home. Alvin had gone back on a horse the next day to collect the money.

"What if I was to trade you a jug of whiskey instead?" Thomas Whisler joked.

"No sir, Mr. Whisler. I got to have the money."

"Shit, make it two jugs. Or"—Thomas Whisler threw his head back and laughed—"does your preacher pa drink likker?"

They stood in the yard near a pen where two mules were happily chomping on the fodder. Young Bailey was carrying his prized pistol in a holster strapped around his waist, but it didn't occurr to him right then to use it. "I got to have the money, Mr. Whisler."

"How about I give you a kick in the ass instead? Send you down the road a-talkin' to yourself."

"Pop said to get the money."

"Well, you go on back home and tell your papa I ain't got the money and I'll pay him when I git damned good and ready." Whisler laughed again. "Tell him to ask his savior for it. Haw-haw."

The boy didn't know what to do. He hated to go back without the money, but it looked as if he'd have to. Well, he'd try again. "Mr. Whisler, Pop ain't gonna like you promising to pay and not paying."

"What's he gonna do about it? Pray for my soul? Haw-haw. Now you git on down the road. Hear?"

"Mr. Whisler, uh . . ."

Rough hands grabbed the boy by the shoulders and spun him around. A size twelve boot kicked him in the seat of the pants so hard that he fell and skinned his hands on the rocky ground. It was the last thing Thomas Whisler ever did.

The big Army Colt boomed and a .44 ball hit the bearded hulk squarely in the heart. He flopped onto his back, kicked once, and died.

At home, Alvin told everyone what he'd done, and the

Bailey family stayed up most of the night praying. They prayed for Mr. Whisler's soul, but mostly they prayed for Alvin. He'd taken a life. But Alvin felt no shame, no regret. How could Thomas Whisler have been so dumb as to kick a boy who was carrying a gun?

The killing had to be reported to the law, but not before the boy had saddled a horse, tied a blanket roll behind the cantle, and was headed west to Mount Capulin, where his dad's brother lived. He carried a loaf of bread, a small iron skillet, and a pound of cured bacon. And his prized pistol. The Bailey family had had too many bad experiences with the law in East Texas and they were taking no chances.

At fourteen, Alvin Charles Bailey was a killer and a fugitive. By the time he reached twenty, he'd killed a dozen men.

Now he was about to kill again.

He was still smiling that half smile when he deliberately looked beyond the short cowboy to the corral. "That black horse 'pears to be a good mount. I'll take him and call it even. That is, if you'll go get my saddle for me."

"Nothin' doin'. I'm marchin' you over to Taos to the laws. If you make one wrong move, I'll shoot the shit out of you. Maybe I'll get a ree-ward."

"You don't say." Ace Bailey was still relaxed, still smiling.

"Shuck that gun." The cowboy's eyes were narrow, wary.

"Well," Ace drawled, looking to the southeast, "you won't have to march very far. The sheriff is coming over here."

For a split second, the cowboy's eyes shifted toward Taos. Only a split second. Ace Bailey threw himself to the right and down, drawing and firing before he hit the ground. The cowboy's big pistol boomed, but the bullet tore a hole in the sky. He was falling. A .38 slug had hit him on the left side of the nose, ripping out through his right ear.

Standing and holstering the pearl-handled Colt. Bailey murmured to the dead man, "Now I'll have to take the horse and your saddle."

14

He saddled the black gelding went inside the shack, and yanked a tarp off the dead man's bed. The bigger of the skillets was still too hot to handle, so he settled for a small one, another sack of coffee, and more jerky. With the items rolled up in the tarp, he went outside and noticed a half-dozen townsmen coming cautiously across the vacant lot to see what the shooting had been all about. He ignored the group until he had the tarp and its contents tied behind the cantle, then he turned and faced them.

"Morning, gents," he said pleasantly.

They stared at the dead man and at Bailey, standing there as if petrified. Finally, a thin man with a bill cap on his head spoke haltingly. "Are you . . . are you Ace Bailey?"

"Yup." Bailey swung into the saddle. "Tell everybody that he tried to cheat me at the point of a gun. And tell the laws I'll see them in Albukirk." Reining the black, he rode north, leaving the townsmen wondering what to do.

At the spot where he'd spent the night, Ace changed saddles and picked up the longest piece of the rope. He had to decide whether to take the coffeepot or the skillet. A man could carry just so much behind a cantleboard. The coffeepot was the best bet, he decided. Hell, he had nothing to fry in the skillet, anyway. He rode down the narrow path to the bottom of the Rio Grande gorge and wondered if he had made a mistake. The path up the other side was narrow, rocky, and steep. Those Mexican burros could make it, but a horse? "Whatta you think, feller?" he asked the black. Shaking his head sadly, he apologized, "Wish I didn't have to do this to you, but I ain't got time to go back. Maybe it'd help if I got down and walked."

Dismounting, he walked, leading the horse. As they started up the west side, the animal balked. Bailey talked quietly. "Don't blame you, pardner. Shame to hurt a good horse. But we got to go on." He pulled the horse a step to the left, then a step to the right, then ahead up the path. It followed. A misstep would have been fatal to the animal. A man could roll downhill without getting hurt, but not a horse. At places, the animal almost ran over Bailey, wanting to get to the top and get this hard work over with. "Easy, feller. Save your wind."

As they climbed Ace kept looking back, thinking about what a good target he'd make climbing out of the gorge. There was nothing to take cover behind. He'd be a sitting duck. And a dead one. Badly winded himself, he climbed. At one spot where there was room, he tossed the reins over the horse's neck and stepped aside, letting the animal go on past. That might be dumb, he said under his breath. The horse would be impossible to catch up there. But he thought it would have a better chance of making it to the top with him out of the way. He climbed, at times hand over hand. What would he do if the horse fell? He'd be afoot unless he could find a Mexican farmer with a horse he could buy. He had money, winnings from a horse race back at Las Vegas. It was because of that horse race that he was running again.

That was day before yesterday. This was now.

Looking up, he saw a shale ledge break under the horse's forefeet, saw it scramble for another toehold, hump, and buck. "Atta boy," he said aloud. Finally, the animal was on top, walking away. Two minutes later Ace Bailey was on top, standing on unsteady legs, breathing hard. Looking back, he was relieved to see no one on the other side. Either the lawmen hadn't gotten that far or they'd found an easier place to cross the gorge.

"Okay," Bailey puffed. "Now let's see if I can catch that horse."

It turned out to be easy. While the black grazed on the high country grass, the reins slid off its neck to the ground. After stepping on the reins twice, it stood still. Bailey walked up, took hold of the reins near the bit, and backed the horse a step to get its left hind foot off the end of a rein, then climbed into the saddle. He rode west a mile, hoping to fool anyone who might be tracking him, then swung north back to the river, climbing steadily. He was in tall timber now, up where he could look down on the Taos Valley and the sagebrush flats. Still climbing, he found a rocky but shallow crossing and again put the horse

16

through the waters of the Rio Grande.

"*Adios,* Mr. River, and good-bye," he said aloud.

When he broke into open country, he could again see down into the valley. Still no bunch of riders hot on his trail. Maybe the law dogs hadn't gotten as far as Arroyo Hondo, or maybe they didn't like the looks of the gorge and had gone back south, hoping to catch him at Albuquerque. Turning east, he looked for the wagon road that climbed from Taos all the way up to Eagle Nest, then down into the Cimarron River Canyon. Sister Mindy lived in the tiny town of Cimarron. She'd married a Cornishman who'd come to the territory to work in the silver mines but decided he'd rather be outside. Ace could stay a while at Mindy's. He reckoned Eagle Nest was two days away and Cimarron was another day, but he was in no hurry now.

Near the road he offsaddled and let the black graze on the mountain grass while he chewed more of the jerky. "I might shrink a few pounds before I get my next good meal," he mused aloud, "but this'll keep me alive." Before dark, he reined off the road a mile and made camp. He had to cut a strip off the bed tarp to use for hobbles. Tonight he had a fire and coffee, and while he was sipping it he used the coffeepot to boil some of the jerky. That made it a little easier to chew.

At sunup he was horseback again, still going north, up-hill. The black was a good horse, strong with good wind.

"Where were you when that sonofabitch traded me the grey horse?" Bailey asked. He got no answer. "He must've had you hid where I couldn't see you. If I'd seen you I would've traded for you, and that jasper would still be alive." Riding on, he spoke to himself. "How many have I killed now." Thirteen? Yeah, that's how many. That's an unlucky number. I don't like thirteen of anything. No sir, I don't like that number."

At the top of a hill, just before the road dipped into a broad, pine-studded valley, he saw a string of wagons about a mile away coming from the opposite direction. It wouldn't do for him to be seen. The wagons were no doubt headed for Taos, and any lawmen who happened to be there would ask the teamsters if they'd seen a man on a black horse.

Nope, got to get out of sight. He turned the horse back downhill, off the road, and booted it into a lope for a mile, where they came to a thick growth of spruce and pine. Back among the trees, out of sight, he reined up. "Hope they didn't see me. Don't think they did. Can't take a gamble right now."

He rode on, going north, but far east of the Rio Grande. What he hoped to find was another trail going over the mountains. Surely, he thought, someone had found a way from here — Indians, prospectors, somebody. A half mile from the forest, he was almost ready to give up. There was no sign that anyone else in the whole damned world had ever been over this way. But ahead was a rocky knoll, and from there he figured he ought to have a good view of the surrounding country. He turned the black in that direction, thinking that if he saw nothing from there he'd wait a while and go back to the wagon road.

At the top of the knoll he sat his horse for a long moment, scanning the terrain in all directions. To the east was a timbered ridge that seemed to stretch clear across the horizon. Back the way he had come was a notch in the ridge, and that had to be where the wagon road crossed it. All right, he'd wait until the wagon train had had plenty of time to get out of sight, then go back. Meantime, his stomach was growling.

Sitting on the ground, chewing jerked beef, he watched the horse graze and let his eyes settle on a strange-looking stone twenty feet ahead of him. Odd. It had a hole in it and grass was growing out of the hole. Curious, he stood and walked over, reaching down for it. Bailey drew back.

It was a human skull.

18

Three

"Huh?" Ace Bailey snorted. "What in holy hell . . ."

Now that he was looking, he found more bones. Human bones. Another skull. Another. A rib cage. And in a clump of tall grass there were dried, rotting leather saddles. Four of them. Near one of the skulls he found a dozen empty rimfire cartridges. And still more bones. Some of them had hooves. Horses.

Fascinated, Ace Bailey walked all over the knoll, studying the bones and the rusty cartridge shells. He didn't see the frying pan nearly covered with dirt until he stepped on one edge of it. It flipped up and banged him on the ankle, making him jump as if he'd been struck by a rattlesnake. "Huh," he grunted, surprised and scared. Glancing down, he half expected to see a ghostly hand grabbing at him. His breath came out with a relieved sigh when he picked up the pan.

"Huh," he grunted again. "If anything else jumps up around here, I'm gonna be hard to catch." Moving cautiously now, he picked up a pistol near one of the human skulls, a heavy hunk of rust with a Colt-type extractor rod. Near it he picked up a dried and twisted leather boot. Bones covered with parched skin dropped out.

"Good Gawdamighty," he muttered. "At least four men and some horses, wiped out." Now that he had studied it, he figured out what had happened. There was a circle of rocks, no more than knee high. The

19

rocks had been scattered some and grass was growing among them, but he could see that they had been piled there by human hands. A fortress. Sure. What else? Four men and some horses killed by Indians. They'd put up a battle. Squatting, looking closely at the ground, Bailey found more rimfire cartridges. A lot of shots had been fired. The knoll and its little fortress of rocks was a good place to fight off an Indian attack. But, Bailey guessed, there had been only four men. No telling how many Indians. "I'll bet," he mused, "the goddamn redskins paid a price." He guessed it would be useless to look for Indian bones. Indians usually carried off their dead.

Who were they? And how long ago had it happened? Had any of the white men gotten away?

When he thought about it, he knew some of the answers. He'd found no arrows, which meant the Indians had had guns. And the guns had fired metallic cartridges. That meant it had happened not too awful long ago. And no white man had escaped. If so, he would have come back with some help to pick up the bodies of his partners. As to who they were, Bailey found no clue. Travelers, probably, going down to Taos or coming from Taos. Spotted by a bunch of Apaches or Comanches who hated white-eyes.

"Well," Bailey said, looking down at a half-buried human rib cage, "rest in peace. Me, I think I'll haul my bones away from here in case your spirits don't like my company."

Back on the wagon road, he kept his eyes constantly on the horizon, not wanting to meet any travelers. An hour before dark, he spotted a few log buildings on a wide windswept vega. One of the buildings had a high false front, and Bailey guessed it was a general store. Angel, the place was called. Bailey had heard of it. He guessed it was named Angel because it was so high in the mountains that it was close to heaven.

20

"I could sure use some chuck from that store," he said to the horse, "but best stay away from there." Riding wide around Angel, he went on until he was in the timber again. There he stopped for the night, wishing he had another blanket to keep him warm in the high, thin, chilly air. For a moment he considered going back to the store he'd seen, but only for a moment. "If I want to get old," he said to himself, "I can't let my stomach do my thinking for me." He made his meal of coffee and boiled jerky, wrapped the bed tarp and blanket around himself, and tried to sleep. Around two o'clock he had to stand, stomp his feet, and wave his arms to get warm. Looking at the stars, seemingly so close he could almost reach up and grab one, he muttered, "What the hell do you think this is, December? Hell, it's goddamn August, goddamnit." Finally, he lay back down and slept fitfully.

It was past noon when he came to Eagle Nest. Another cluster of log buildings stood near the edge of a small lake, and he had to go out of his way to keep from being seen. Then, with the warm mid-afternoon sun making the horse sweat, he stopped on top of the divide and looked down behind him. "I'll bet it's colder than a witch's tit up here in the winter. I'll bet the snow's ass-deep to a tall Indian." Looking ahead, he said to the horse, "We still got a ways to go, feller, but it's downhill from here."

Camp that night was on the edge of a vega, where the horse had plenty of grass to graze on. It was another cold, hungry night for Ace Bailey. "This running from the law can get someone old in a hurry," he groused to himself. Shortly after daylight they were traveling again, following the wagon road.

At one time, just before noon, he had to get off the road and hide behind some huge boulders while six freight wagons went by, and an hour later he had to hide while a light buggy pulled by two horses passed. A man and woman were in the buggy. A rancher and his wife, probably. Then he was in the canyon of the Cimarron River, looking up at eight-hundred-foot-high cliffs of yellowish rock. The cliffs were lined with perpendicular cracks caused by the earth's movement over thousands of years. The river gurgled happily, clean and pure, between huge cottonwood trees, pine, spruce, willows, and buck brush. "A good place to camp, pardner, but if we keep going we can get to Cimarron by dark. If I don't get something besides jerked beef in my guts pretty soon, you'll be packing a dead man."

It was dusk when he rode into the village called Cimarron. Feeling a little weak now from hunger, Bailey stopped beside a man in bib overalls and asked if he knew of a Cornishman named Jack Wembley who had a wife named Mindy.

"Cousin Jack?" the man said. "Shore. Over yonder just under that big hill. It's a plank house with a split shingle roof. You a kin of his?"

"Yeah," Bailey said. "Obliged."

At the door of the two-room house, Bailey stayed on his horse and hollered, "Jack? Mindy?"

It was the big blond Cornishman who opened the door and looked out. His weathered face was puzzled at first, then his eyes widened. "Damn, man, you ain't . . . are you Alvin?"

"I'd reckon," Bailey drawled, "that you're Jack, the gent that married my kid sister."

The Cornishman's face split into a grin. "Alvin." Looking back inside, he said. "Mindy, look who's here." Then his young sister was in the doorway, smiling and crying at the same time. "Alvin, thank God. I've been trying to locate you. Get down and let Jack take care of your horse. Come in. I've got bad news."

The big blond Jack took the reins and led the horse to a corral behind the house, while Bailey followed his sister inside. The house consisted of a kitchen and a bedroom. A cast-iron cookstove sat near the door, and a table and four chairs, homemade from rough-hewn lumber, occupied the middle of the room. Cabinets, two made of the same kind of lumber and two made of grocery crates, had been nailed to a wall near the stove.

"Sit down, Alvin." He sat in one of the chairs and she sat across the table. "You look peak-ud. Are you running again?"

Sister Mindy was a pretty girl, with the same straw-colored hair, high cheekbones, and a firm chin. Slender, but now pregnant. She was eighteen.

"You said something about bad news, Mindy?"

"Yes, Alvin." Sniffling, blinking back tears, she went on. "Something terrible happened. I've been trying to find you and tell you. Mom needs you. Pop needs you. Jim is dead."

"Jim?" Bailey's stomach suddenly went hollow. His throat tightened. He had to squeeze the words out. "How? What?"

"They hung him. They came in the middle of the night. A mob of them. They took him outside and hung him from the barn loft. They told Pop they would hang him too if he didn't get out of the country."

"What? Why?" Speaking was almost impossible. "Because of . . . of me?"

"No. Some cattle was stolen and they said Jim was doing the stealing. They think Pop was stealing, too."

"But that's . . . that's not so. Jim . . . Pop . . . they never stole anything."

Tears were running down Mindy's face now, but suddenly she wiped her nose with the back of a hand and wiped her eyes. "Of course it's not so. That sheriff and his band of cutthroats were mad because they couldn't find out who was doing it, and they just had to hang somebody."

Anger was replacing the shock inside Ace Bailey, and his voice trembled with it. "It was because of me. Be-

23

cause of me they think the whole Bailey family is bad."

She reached across the table and touched his clenched fist. "Don't blame yourself, Alvin. Nobody in the family blames you. You turned out the way you did because of" — she had to think of a way to say it — "because of the way things are."

Standing, he stomped across the room, turned, then stomped back. "The sheriff, you say? Who's sheriff now?"

"A man named Petersen. Cecil Petersen, I think."

"How did you find out about this?"

"Uncle Amos came over from Capulin and told me. I went home and stayed with Mom and Pop a few days. You've been gone so long. We heard you were cowboying in Texas somewhere, but we didn't know where."

"Yeah, I . . . uh . . . I've been around some. I should have been at home. I should have been there. Jim, he was a good man and he'd fight if he had to but he . . . he'd take a lot before he believed he had to. Pop . . . Pop believes in turning the other cheek like it says in the Bible."

"Mom said she's thankful you weren't there, because there was so many of them they'd have hung you, too."

"Petersen, huh? I want to meet that gentleman."

"No, don't, Alvin. He's always got a bunch of men with guns around him. They'll kill you."

"I have to go home. I have to see Mom and Pop."

"Yes, but be careful. They know what you look like."

Heavy boots stomping up to the door stopped their conversation. Jack opened the door slowly and put his big shaggy head in carefully, as if he didn't want to interrupt his wife and her brother. When he saw they were not talking, he came in. "Your black horse is havin' a bally good time with that Injun corn," he said, smiling. "That bloomin' blanket roll of yours is too skinny. You can't have much to eat in it. Mindy was gonna cook some supper and she'll fill your belly."

24

Smiling a weak smile, Bailey said, "Speaking of bellies, I don't know anything about women, Mindy, but it looks like you're in foal."

"Yes." She smiled that pretty smile he remembered well. "In about a month, we figure."

"I'm gonna be an uncle. Won't that be something? Is there a doctor in these parts?"

"No, but there's Mrs. Jackson. She's had a lot of experience delivering babies."

"Fine, fine . . . uh . . ." Bailey's smile slowly vanished, "Have the laws around here ever asked about me?"

"No, Alvin. No one here knows I'm your sister. You're safe here."

"Stay as long as you want to, Alvin, old son," Jack said. "We'll make you a bed on the kitchen floor."

Standing, Mindy said, "I'll fix some supper. Alvin, you do look peak-ud. How long since you had a good meal?"

They ate roast venison, boiled potatoes, carrots, and homemade bread. They finished the meal with canned peaches. Ace leaned back in his chair with a contented sigh. "I think I'll live now."

"It does appear you've got some color in your face after all."

"Uncle Amos tells me you're working at a sawmill, Jack?"

"Sure. I got the bloody coughs and strangles muckin' in those bally mines in Colorada, and I come down here to get some clean air in my lungs."

"He's making us a good living, Alvin."

Dishes washed, they sat at the table and talked. Jack smoked a long-stemmed pipe. When the conversation got around to Jim, the young woman's eyes filled with tears again. Ace patted her on the shoulder and struggled to keep his own emotions under control. Jack excused himself and went into the bedroom, leaving brother and sister to console each other.

Later, lamps blown out, Ace was comfortable on a pallet on the kitchen floor. Before he dozed off he knew he was going to have to kill another man. A man with a sheriff's badge. That would make it fourteen.

Well, hell, he didn't like the number thirteen anyway.

Four

The black horse needed at least two days rest before it was ready to continue the journey. Bailey believed it would take two long days to get home, three if he stopped at Uncle Amos's near Mount Capulin. "Take some bacon and bread with you," his sister said. "And some canned peaches. You look like your bones was hung on you with spiderwebs."

Grinning, Bailey allowed, "I don't care if I never see another strip of jerked beef. Nothing but dogs can chew that stuff."

"The bally dogs and the bally Mexes," Jack quipped.

He left early in the morning, the black horse carrying him, a blanket roll, and saddlebags stuffed with groceries. He headed the horse in the direction he believed Mount Capulin to be, figuring to stay south of Raton. The country here was flat, and the horse jogged along at a steady pace through yucca, cane cactus, and sagebrush. The Raton Mountains rose in a jagged purple line far to the north, and the flat-topped mesas, capped with erosion-resistant shale, lay ahead.

Before noon, he crossed the deeply rutted Santa Fe trail, abandoned now that the railroad had reached Santa Fe. By mid afternoon, he could see the huge cinder cone called Mount Capulin, and he knew he wouldn't get to his uncle's small ranch that day. "It's farther than I thought it was," he said to the horse. "Guess we'd better find a place to camp before dark."

27

He made camp in a shallow draw where he had to break off sagebrush to burn. Believing he was safe here, and knowing sagebrush burned fast and left no hot coals for cooking, he kept the fire going. A skillet loaded with bacon sat in the middle of it. Dusk came by the time the bacon was fried, and he let the fire die. Sitting on the ground, eating bacon and bread, watching the horse graze in the dusk, he heard a sound that made his blood freeze. It came from behind him, and there was no mistaking what it was.

It was the ratcheting sound of a gun being cocked.

Ace Bailey froze, afraid to move, his mind racing. Who was it? Was he going to die right here? There was no other sound. Did he dare turn his head and look back? For a long moment he sat still, looking straight ahead. Then, forcing calmness into his voice, he asked, "Are you gonna shoot me in the back? Who are you and what do you want?"

"Take that pistol out of its holster and throw it away." The voice was strange, a little high-pitched. A kid. But it was a hard voice. The speaker meant business.

"Who are you?"

"Never mind. Do like I said, or you'll never know what hit you."

"You wouldn't shoot a man in the back, would you?" He was using time, trying to find a way out of the fix he was in.

"You're durn tootin' I would. Now, do like I said, or I'm gonna blow your head off."

"Is it money you want? My horse?" His mind was racing, desperate.

"You'll find out. No, I reckon you won't, because I'm gonna shoot. I'll give you one more second to do like I said. And be durned careful how you do it."

There was no way out. Whoever was behind Ace had him in his gunsights. No matter how fast he moved, he couldn't grab the Colt, turn, and find his target fast enough. Slowly, he pulled the Colt .38 out of the holster with two fingers and tossed it aside. "Now what?"

"Don't move 'til I tell you to." Footsteps. The kid stepped around him, between Ace and the dying fire. He wore baggy bib overalls, a wide-brimmed hat, and brogan shoes. He had no gunbelt, but he had a lever-action rifle pointed at Bailey.

"Who are you and what do you want?" Bailey asked again.

"Who are you and what're you doin' here?"

"My name is . . . uh . . . Alvin, and I'm traveling. Why don't you point that damned gun somewhere else?"

Slowly, the rifle barrel was lowered, but the hammer was still back, and the gun could be brought up and fired in an instant. "What're you doin' over here?"

"I'm traveling straight for Capulin Mountain, and I don't need a road to find my way. Say"—he squinted at the kid in the near darkness—"you . . . uh . . . good God, you're a woman!"

"So what? I can shoot as fast and straight as you can."

"Well, I'll be damned. Durned. Now let me ask you. What're you doing here?"

"Traveling. Same as you."

"Well, are you gonna point a gun at everybody you meet?"

"Everybody I meet way out in the tullies like this."

"You could have just gone on around, you know. Why didn't you?"

"I ran out of groceries, and I smelled bacon frying."

Bailey eyed his Colt lying on the ground not far away. Maybe he could distract the woman long enough to grab it and shoot. But naw, he didn't want to shoot her. He'd never shot a woman and he didn't intend to. Besides, he was curious as hell. "Well, put that smoke pole away, and I'll build up the fire and fry some more bacon."

She was hesitant. "You . . . you wouldn't harm a woman, would you?"

"Not unless she keeps threatening to shoot me."

"Well, a woman alone has to be careful."

"Yeah, you're prob'ly right. Now, do you want me to get up and get the fire going again?"

"All right, but I'm keeping this rifle cocked and ready."

Groping in the dark, Ace broke off more sagebrush, piled it on what remained of his fire, then got on his knees and blew on it until he got a blaze going. Ignoring the woman, he broke up more sagebrush and sliced some bacon. She put her rifle on the ground while she ate with her fingers. Her hands had short fingernails, but they were not the work-worn hands of a laboring woman. Ace knew he could grab her rifle or his six-gun, but he chose not to.

"Where are you traveling to?" he asked. "And how come you're traveling horseback instead of in a coach?"

"None of your business."

He had to chuckle at that. "Well, you'd better bring your horse over here and get him unsaddled and hobbled, or he ain't gonna carry you very far."

"I know how to take care of a horse. How far is it to Cimarron?"

"If you leave at daylight, you'll get there before dark."

"What if I spend the night here? You wouldn't try to take advantage of a woman, would you?"

Chuckling again, Ace said, "Well, I'm no gentleman, as anybody in the territory can tell you, but I've never taken advantage of a woman. For that matter, I've never taken an unfair advantage of a man."

"What did you say your name is?"

"Alvin. Alvin Bailey. Now, what's your name?"

30

"Stewart, Marybelle Stewart. I've heard your name somewhere, I think. Are you a kin of Ace Bailey?"

"I've met him. Let me ask you again. What are you doing here?"

"I . . . it's none of your business."

"If I had to guess," Bailey chuckled, "I'd say you're either running from somebody or looking for somebody."

"I'm not running from anybody." When he stared at her in the dim firelight, she added, "I'm looking for somebody."

"Oh. Now I understand."

She stopped licking bacon grease from her fingers long enough to snap, "No, you don't."

"You're right, I don't. Uh . . . I'd guess you came from Raton, but if you did, how come you don't follow the road? It's easier to travel on."

"That's none of your business."

"Oh, I understand."

"No, you don't understand." She stood and went to fetch her horse, a rangy bay. Bailey stayed where he was and watched her unsaddle and hobble the animal. After she'd carried a blanket roll back to the fire and was seated on the ground again, she took off her hat, letting thick, rich chestnut hair fall to her shoulders. Squinting at her in the semidarkness, Bailey saw a face that was weathered, with a hint of hardness in the hazel eyes. Still, she was a handsome woman, maybe in her early thirties. She was a woman who had not had an easy life but had taken pride in her face and figure.

Yeah, the carefully shaped eyebrows and the long hair that had been combed and brushed often were proof of that. He'd seen her kind in the saloons. They tried to maintain a youthful appearance, but they were destined to turn hard. Hard and bitter.

The two sat in silence while the fire burned itself out. Then, out of the darkness, she said, "I know you

31

could have grabbed your gun."

"Well, if you don't mind, I believe I'll put it back where it belongs." Bailey stood and picked up the gun. He holstered it and sat again.

"The man I'm looking for didn't follow any road."

"Then he was running."

"I'm not saying any more."

"Was he alone?"

"No, there were four of them."

"Four of them? Running from the law?"

"I'm not saying any more."

"When was this?" In his mind, Bailey could see the human bones on top of a knoll somewhere south and west of Eagle Nest Lake.

"A long time ago."

"How come you're just now looking for them?"

"I've looked before."

"Must be pretty important. How come you're not looking in the towns?"

"I've looked in the towns. I've been to Taos, Santa Fe, Albuquerque, El Paso, and all the settlements in between. Nobody ever saw them."

"So now you're searching the hills."

"Yes, I know my chances are practically zero, but like you said, it's important."

"How come?"

"I'm not saying any more."

With a shrug, Bailey stood and picked up his tarp and blanket. "You're right, it's none of my business. I'm gonna try to get some shut-eye. I've got some traveling to do." He carried his bed out of sight and unrolled it on a stretch of bare ground. After he'd pulled off his boots, lain on the blanket, and covered himself with the tarp, he heard her moving in the dark, doing the same. For a while he lay awake, wondering about the woman. She had to have wanted to find the four men very badly to go riding all over the country like this. He was almost certain the four were long dead and all she would find were their bones. Should he tell her about it? Yeah, sure, why not? He'd tell her in the morning.

Five

Marybelle Stewart was up before he was, and from somewhere in her saddlebags or blanket roll, she had produced a long comb and was using it on her shoulder-length chestnut hair. In the daylight her oval face, full lips, and perfect eyebrows made her even more attractive. The baggy bib overalls hid her figure, but Bailey could see she was neither overweight nor skinny. When she had her hair combed, she piled it on top of her head and tucked it under the high-crown hat.

They talked little as he built a fire, fried bacon, and sliced bread. Not until after they'd eaten and saddled their horses did Bailey ask, "So you're going to Cimarron, Gonna keep looking, are you?"

With a resigned shrug, she said, "Yes, For a few days, anyway."

"Maybe I can make it easier."

The eyebrows went up. "How?"

"It's bad news."

"Do you know something about my father?"

"Your father?" When she nodded, he looked down at his boots and wondered again whether he should tell her.

"Well. Do you?"

"Maybe."

"Well, tell me."

All right, he had to tell her now. "Uh . . . Miss Stewart, I came across some human bones back up there." He nodded toward the southwest. "There were four men and some horses, Prob'ly killed by Indians."

"Where?" She paled a moment, then looked hard at him.

He tried to tell her. "It's about ten miles south of Eagle Nest Lake and about two or two and a half miles west of the wagon road. It's on a little hill out in the open country. If you get within a quarter mile of it, you'll see it."

"There are skeletons of four men?"

"Yeah, Think they're the ones you're looking for?"

Her face showed interest, a lot of interest. Excitement had crept into her voice. "It might be. It very well could be. Can you give me any better directions than that?"

Shaking his head, Bailey said, "I don't know what else to tell you. I doubt if I could go right to it myself. I'd have to look for it."

"Can you take me there?"

"Naw, I've got to get home."

"I'll pay you."

"Wish I could, but I've got to see my folks."

"It's worth a lot to me. I'll pay you well."

"Oh? How come it's worth so much?"

"Well, I . . . I . . . uh . . . want to give my father a decent burial."

Bailey studied her face, knowing she wasn't telling the whole truth but unable to guess at what the whole truth was. Finally, he said, "Well, Miss Stewart, if you do enough riding, you'll find it. If you don't, maybe you can get somebody that runs cattle in that country to help you."

"Yes, I'll . . . I'll stay in Cimarron tonight and buy some groceries, then go on tomorrow."

Bailey mounted his horse. "Good luck."

"Yes. Thanks for the grub."

He rode away without looking back.

Alvin Charles Bailey had been sixteen when he'd earned his reputation as a very dangerous man. He'd spent nearly a year with his bachelor uncle Amos, who ran a few cattle

35

and farmed a few acres where a spring came out of the Raton Mountains. They worked, played cards, and competed with each other at shooting tin cans. A.C. had a talent for it. And he liked to shoot. He liked the feel of the recoil, the noise, and he liked to see a tin can jump or a glass jar shatter when his bullet hit where he aimed.

At fifteen he rolled up his blankets and rode north to the railroad town of Trinidad, in the new state of Colorado. For a time he worked in a coal mine days and played cards nights in the El Raton saloon. Mining wasn't his kind of work, and eventually he was spending his time playing cards. Turned out he had a talent for that, too. In fact, he'd gamble on almost anything.

Anything but cockfights.

As a boy, he'd raised some red chickens at home. He fed them grain from the Indian corn and they got to know him, especially a big red rooster. Though chickens were among the most stupid creatures on earth, he liked having the rooster jump onto his knee as he sat on the ground and eat out of his hand. The Bailey family had to kill chickens to eat, but no one dared touch that rooster.

Now here was a circle of men whooping and cheering wildly while two roosters cut each other to pieces.

It was sickening. The two dozen men were sickening, the way they yelled for blood. The bloodier the fight, the more they cheered. Bailey watched one fight and turned to leave. But no sooner were the two dead or dying cocks picked up than two more were put in the ring. Money was changing hands rapidly. Whoops, yells, cheers, as the two roosters cut each other with the man-made spurs on their feet. Blood was flying.

Two quick shots put the chickens out of their misery.

By the time the men realized what had happened, the kid nicknamed Ace was backing away, a six-gun in his hand.

"Anybody tries to stop me gets the next bullet," he said.

One man grabbed for the six-gun on his hip. He fell

dead with a .44 ball in his heart. The rest stood still, shocked.

Bailey went back home to Stockwell County then. He stayed away from town, and no one outside his family knew he was there. He hoed Johnson grass in the fields, helped harvest the maize and sweet corn, and fed the chickens. Then one day he believed he'd stayed away from the rest of the world long enough, and went to town with his mother and dad. That was the day the three J's met their deaths.

They were Jasper Short, Jason Hammer, and James Wilheim, three veterans of the war between the states who had a few cattle and a plowed field six miles west of the town of Stockwell. The three never shaved and seldom changed clothes, and everywhere they went they carried big pistols in low-slung holsters. Somehow their cows all had twin calves and some of their steers wore fresh Triple J brands. The plowed field was overgrown with weeds. The three were always well fed with beef, and they never butchered their own.

Everyone knew they were thieves, but no one dared call them that to their faces. Especially after they'd killed two men in separate saloon brawls. The Stockwell County sheriff tried twice to arrest them, but both times he lost a deputy to their deadly guns.

When they started hoo-rawing the Reverend Bailey that day, they were just having their kind of fun. They didn't pay any attention to the sixteen-year-old boy who'd come to town with the Baileys.

"Hey, Parson," said the one named Jason, "how's about givin' us a sermon. Haw-haw."

The Reverend and Mrs. Bailey had climbed down from their wagon and were about to go into the Stockwell Mercantile. The boy was horseback. Two of the J's, full of cheap whiskey, had just come out of the mercantile.

"Come on, now, savin' souls is your callin', ain't it?"

"Haw-haw. Give us some a' that hell's fire and stuff."

37

"Shore. Git back on that wagon and preach your goddamn head off. Us sinners need to hear some preachin'."

The two J's didn't notice the kid getting down from his horse.

The Reverend Bailey looked from one J to the other and said, "Come to our church Sunday, and I'll be happy to deliver a sermon."

"Not Sunday. Now. Haw-haw. Or would you rather listen to this here six-shooter?" Jasper Short fired a shot into the ground near the senior Bailey's feet. The horses started to bolt, but the reverend caught the driving lines and held them back. The kid moved over next to his dad.

"Come on, now. There ain't nothin' to do for fun in this here goddamn town, so give us some hollerin' and footstompin'. Haw-haw." He fired another shot.

An Army Colt appeared in the kid's hand—just suddenly appeared. Fire and smoke belched out the bore. Jasper Short fell in a heap on the street. Jason Hammer grabbed for the six-gun on his hip. The gun didn't clear leather. A second shot from the kid's gun sent him spinning with a bullet in his right side. The third shot knocked him down. James Wilheim came from somewhere, saw his partners down, and thought a posse was after him. He took off, running to his horse tied in front of the saloon. The Army Colt belched fire and smoke again.

The three J's were no more.

The Baileys went home and prayed. "Oh Lord," The reverend's eyes rolled upward, "please help this child to live a peaceful life."

It wasn't to be. The sheriff of Stockwell County knew now that Ace Bailey was at home. But before he could gather a dozen townsmen to go and arrest him, young Bailey was on his way to Texas.

Word spread fast, all over the Territory. Some folks considered Ace Bailey a hero for getting rid of three bullies. Lawmen considered him a killer.

In West Texas he hired on to help drive two thousand

four hundred longhorn cattle to Dodge City. It took nearly three months, and along the way the kid learned how to handle a big herd and how to cross rivers.

Dodge City was wild. Gunfire and fistfights were nightly events. Young Bailey did his share of drinking and gambling and made two trips to the joy houses, but he stayed out of fights. He bought his pearl-handled, silver-plated .38 from a gunsmith in Dodge. It didn't have the boom or recoil of the big Army Colt, but he liked the feel of it and the way he could draw and fire it in a hurry. At the chuck wagon, away from town, Bailey practiced with it until he could hold a tin can waist high on the back of his hand, slip his hand from under it, draw, and shoot before it hit the ground. Other cowboys liked to watch him shoot cans in the air. The way to do it, he found, was to wait until the can had reached its peak and paused a split second before it started to fall, then shoot, Young Bailey seldom missed, and he won some bets. But soon no one would bet with him.

Back home in Stockwell County, Ace and brother Jim counted their money, borrowed from their dad, and decided to build a herd of Texas cattle of their own to drive to Dodge. They bought some horses and went to the Big Bend country in Texas, where cattle ran wild. The rest of that summer and all winter they worked, building a barbed wire fence around five hundred acres, catching and branding wild cattle, and buying more horses. By early spring they had six hundred cattle and enough horses to mount a small crew of cowboys. The cattle were a little gaunt from being confined to a small pasture, and the brothers wanted to be the first on the trail, while the spring grass was green, so the cattle could gain some weight along the way. They hired five men in the town of Big Bend, outfitted a chuck wagon, and started up the trail.

Before they reached Dodge City, Ace Bailey's reputation grew. He killed two more men.

Six

It was south of the Red River that the Bailey brothers' B Bar cattle were joined by a small bunch of range cattle that were grazing near the trail. The range cattle wore what looked like a JB brand. The B Bar crew worked half a day cutting out the strays and driving them far enough away to get their own herd out of sight. Believing they had all the range cattle cut out, they crossed the river late that day and camped on the north side. At noon next day, four well-armed riders came up behind them, and Jim Bailey rode back to meet them.

"We believe," said a heavy-set, square-faced man on a brown horse, "that some of our cattle are in your herd." Jim explained that they had picked up some range cattle, but he thought they had left them all behind.

"We intend to sort through your herd and see for ourselves," the heavy man said, "Kindly throw 'em off the trail and get 'em millin'."

"That takes time, and we ain't got time to spare," Jim said. "But you're welcome to ride along and examine every cow brute we've got. If you see any of yours, we'll help you cut them out."

"Uh-uh." The man shook his head. "We ain't got time to foller you all the way to Dodge. If you don't get 'em millin', we'll do it for you."

"No," Jim insisted. "You've got enough help that you can cut your cattle out of a moving herd. If you ain't, I'll get

40

two of my crew to help you. But we're not stopping 'til sundown."

"Then we'll stop 'em. Come on, boys." The four men rode at a lope to the head of the herd and began turning back the leaders. Ace was near the head and didn't like what he saw. He rode at a trot to the heavy man and demanded to know what he was doing.

"We intend to sort through your herd for some of our cattle."

"Would you be representing the JB brand? We did have to cut out some JB cattle yesterday, and I'm sure we got them all out."

"Well, we'll just have a look-see."

"Suit yourselves, but meantime we're moving. Get out of the way."

"You ain't movin' 'til I say you're movin'." To his men, the heavy one yelled, "Hold 'em up here, boys."

There was that tingling again. It started in Ace Bailey's legs and worked up into his chest. He turned his horse so the heavy man was on his right. With a half smile on his face, he said, "I'm telling you again, get out of the way."

"Who's gonna make us?" The heavy man's right hand dropped to the butt of a six-gun on his hip.

"I am."

"Shit, we can stampede your cattle all over hell. We can—" Those were the last words he ever spoke.

The .38 popped.

The horses all jumped at the sound, but the men were able to control them. All but one. The heavy man slid out of his saddle and fell onto his left shoulder. He rolled over once and died. One of his sidekicks grabbed for a gun, and the .38 popped again. Two men were down.

"Well?" Ace Bailey said, watching the other two.

"Don't shoot, mister. We're just workin' for wages."

"Ride. And don't come back."

"Yessir."

41

"Wait. Take them with you."

"Yessir."

After the gunfire, the B Bar crew had to do some hard riding themselves to get the herd gathered. When the cattle were finally strung out again, Ace rode back to his brother.

"Them two will fetch the laws, Jim. It ain't much farther to Dodge. Can you handle it without me?"

"I reckon, Alvin. Where are you going?"

"I don't know. You and Pop can keep my share of the profits."

"God be with you, Alvin."

"Yeah. Uh . . . Jim . . . I had to shoot."

"They were looking for a fight."

"So long, Jim. Give my love to Pop and Mama."

Ace Bailey never saw his brother again.

Heading home now, he bypassed Uncle Amos's place, wanting to get home to see his mother and dad. Still, it wasn't until late afternoon the next day that he got there. As he rode up, Ace saw his dad carrying a bucket to the house and knew he'd just milked the Bailey family's cow. "Hyo-o-o," he yelled, standing in the stirrups so he could be seen above the growing corn.

The elder Bailey set the bucket down, squinted into the sun, then hollered, "Alvin." Looking back at the house, he yelled, "Mother, come out here. It's Alvin."

Mrs. Bailey came out onto the back porch, squinted a moment, then let out a shriek and ran into the backyard, holding her arms out. Ace rode up at a lope, bailed off his horse, and wrapped his arms around his mother. Papa Bailey repeatedly slapped his son on the back until Ace turned to him. They shook hands.

Inside the three-room plank house, Mama Bailey's tears of happiness turned to tears of sadness as she told of

42

Jim Bailey's death. "Ever'one knows he didn't have nothin' to do with stealin' no cattle," she said. "But that new sheriff was elected on the promise he'd put a stop to the rustlin' and hang all the rustlers. He had to hang somebody."

"But why Jim?"

The elder Bailey's mouth twisted under a bushy grey moustache. " 'Cause Jim had been going over to Texas to work for a cattleman named Alberts. George Alberts. As soon as Jim suspicioned Alberts was buying stolen cattle, he quit working for him. He didn't snitch on him or anything, just drew his pay and came home. The sheriff—Cecil Petersen is his name—suspicioned Jim was in on the stealing."

"But how about a trial? Didn't Jim get a trial?"

"No. Petersen said he'd get a trial, but a bunch of hooligans busted in the jail, dragged him out, and hung him from a barn loft. The sheriff said he had nothing to do with it. I don't believe him."

"Well, how about the rest of the county? Does anybody else believe him?"

"Some do. Some don't. Most folks I talked to said they don't. But Petersen is the duly elected sheriff."

"Who are these hooligans that did the hanging?"

Mrs. Bailey wiped her eyes with the palms of her hands and said, "They come from Texas, Kansas, or wherever Sheriff Petersen could hire 'em. They're just a bunch of hoodlums."

"However," Papa Bailey put in, "nobody can identify them as the ones that did it. They wore rags around their faces."

Ace Bailey let it all sink in, looking down at the splintery wooden floor, then asked, "Has there been any more cattle rustling since Jim was hung?"

"Sure. Just as much as ever."

"Then everybody ought to know by now that Jim had nothing to do with it."

"They know. There was some talk of getting the county government to call a special election so folks could vote Cecil Petersen out of office, but the talk has died down now."

"I sure wish I could have a palaver with this Cecil Petersen . . . try to find out if he had anything to do with Jim's death."

"You can't, son. He'd know who you are and he'd get his gunslingers to arrest you."

"What has he got against me in Stockwell County?"

"The killing of the three J's. There's a warrant out for your arrest."

"That was a long time ago."

"The warrant's still on the sheriff's desk."

"Do you think if I was arrested and tried I'd be found guilty?"

"I don't think so. There were witnesses to what happened, and those three men were thieves and killers. However, they got a warrant for you anyway."

"Alvin," Mrs. Bailey said, "they can go plumb back to the shootin' of Thomas Whisler if they want to."

Ace didn't say it, but he was thinking: If I'm arrested, word will get out and law officers from several counties will be here with warrants of their own. "Well," he said finally, "I'll try not to get arrested. I'll stay out of sight and help with the work if you need me."

"The weeds is takin' over the cornfield. The maize ain't doin' so good, either. Papa and me, we're thinkin' about sellin' some of this farm. We cain't do all the work our ownselfs."

"I'll stay. If anybody comes along and wonders who I am, tell them I'm a hired hand."

"We sure could use your help, son."

Ace Bailey's heart dropped into his stomach when he saw the way Johnsongrass was outgrowing the corn and maize. The two elderly Baileys had concentrated their la-

44

bor on two acres of carrots and potatoes, hoping to harvest something to eat if nothing else.

"The soil's awful dry," Ace said at the supper table. "How long since it's rained around here?"

"Purt' near two months," Mrs. Bailey said. "We been pumpin' water to irrigate the spuds and carrots, but we cain't pump enough to irrigate the roastin' ears and Indian corn."

"With help from the Lord, we'll save enough to feed our two horses and a couple of hogs," Papa Bailey said. "That's all we can hope for. I'm going to sell our beef cows and their calves. We won't have enough feed for them this winter. We'll keep the milk cow."

Ace labored. He hoed, pumped water out of a long-handled pump in the backyard, and fed the chickens and two hogs. He stayed away from the grazing land where the Baileys had five longhorn cows and four calves. It wouldn't do to meet another rider from a neighboring farm.

While he doctored his blisters with beef tallow, he wished his folks could sell their farm for enough money to quit working. If they did, he could go back to El Paso and play cards, race horses, and find a young woman to sleep with. He'd heard that the city marshal he'd known there was now gone. But as long as his folks needed him here, he'd stay.

El Paso was where Ace Bailey had gone after leaving his brother and a herd of cattle just north of the Red River. He used his talent and luck as a gambler to make a living. El Paso was a tough city where some of the West's most dangerous men liked to hang out, but for a year Ace stayed out of trouble. In a card game he won a sorrel mare that had a reputation for being fast. He ran the mare as often as he could get up a race. The mare lost a few but won more than she lost. Ace Bailey was living well.

When the mare pulled a stifle and could run no more, Ace led her at a slow walk to a nearby ranch and paid the rancher five hundred dollars to feed her well as long as she lived. "I'm gonna come and see her every once in a while," he said, "and if I find her gaunted up, you and me are gonna have something to palaver about."

He was smiling when he said it, but the rancher knew he damned well meant it.

As he aged, Ace Bailey developed into a handsome young man, with his straw-colored hair, straight nose, wide mouth, and square chin. The women he met in the saloons were more than happy to go to bed with him. My God, he thought one night as he rolled over to his side of the bed, I've got everything: money, women, good grub, a big room in a fine hotel, two good horses, and enough luck to keep three men in the chips.

But that all ended when he got into a card game with a sore loser.

It was in the Silver Dollar that it happened. Ace was playing stud with three other men, and the game had been going on for over eighteen hours. All four players were tired and they were getting cranky. All but Ace. His youth gave him more endurance, and he was alert and taking advantage of their weariness. Then a gambler with slicked-back hair and a moustache so thin it appeared to be drawn on with a pencil had two queens and two tens showing. He raised the stakes. Ace had three nines and a deuce showing. He called and raised. The other two players folded. But the dandy, knowing he had queens full and the odds heavily on his side, called and raised. Neither man's face changed expression as each called and raised again. Finally, the dandy had all his money in the center of the table. By now the pot had grown to over twelve hundred greenback dollars. Ace merely called. The dandy hooked his thumbs in the pockets of his brocaded vest, his right

46

hand in position to snatch a nickel-plated pistol out of a shoulder holster. Ace's .38 was on his right hip.

"I put down a lot of money to see what you've got," Ace said. "Let's see 'er."

"Full house," the gambler said, using his left hand to turn up a third queen. "Now don't tell me you got four of a kind."

"Yup." Ace flipped his hole card over. "Just sorry little niners, but there's all four of them."

"I don't believe it." The gambler's eyes were hard. Perspiration was breaking out on his forehead. He looked into the faces of the other two players. "Do you believe that? He palmed that nine. I seen 'im do it."

"Whoa now," Ace said, smiling a half smile. "Just a goddamn minute here. I don't cheat. Now, I'm taking the pot and I'd advise you to keep your insults to yourself." He started raking in the pot with his left hand.

"No, by God, you don't. I'm not lettin' a young pup like you palm cards on me." The nickel-plated pistol appeared in the gambler's hand.

At the same instant, a .38 caliber cartridge exploded with a loud pop under the table.

The gambler's mouth flew open. His eyes widened in surprise. He tried to summon enough strength to point his pistol at Ace, but the .38 fired again, this time above the table.

Without saying a word, without looking at the dead man sprawled with his face on the table and his arms hanging at his sides, Ace Bailey gathered the U. S. government greenbacks. He separated them according to denomination, stuffing some into a shirt pocket and the rest in a pants pocket. Just as he left, he said quietly, "Men that can't stand to lose shouldn't ought to ever gamble. See you gents."

He was in bed in his hotel when a loud knock on the door brought him awake. He stepped into his pants, palmed the .38, went to the door, and asked, "Who's there?"

"It's Marshal Duggan. Mr. Bailey, you're under arrest."

Ace Bailey had wanted no fight with a lawman, and he allowed the marshal to lock him in the city jail. About noon the next day, he was taken before a magistrate who set bail at one thousand dollars. Ace put up the money in cash. But a few days later, it was returned to him. The prosecuting attorney, after having his assistant investigate, decided he could not win a conviction. Everyone had the right of self-defense.

The marshal, however, had sworn to clean up the city, and he ordered Ace Bailey out of town.

"You want to try and run me off," Ace said, facing the marshal on a plank sidewalk in front of the Silver Dollar.

Marshal Duggan knew now he was challenging a very dangerous man. His voice wasn't too steady, but he got the words out. "I don't have to exchange gunfire with you, Bailey. I . . . can get all the help I need."

"If anybody gets killed, Marshal, you'll be among the first."

The marshal, a middle-aged man with flat cheekbones, a wide-brimmed hat, and a Smith and Wesson sitting high on his right hip, glanced around at the small crowd that had gathered. He swallowed hard and said, "If we see you around here day after tomorrow, we'll arrest you again." With that, he turned on his heels and walked rapidly down the sidewalk to his office.

"Whatta you gonna do, Ace?" someone asked.

"Well," Bailey drawled, "I think I'll stick around for a few days to see what happens. Anybody want a game of cards?"

He stayed in El Paso five more days and made sure everyone, including the marshal, saw him. But he knew he was being foolish. Sooner or later, the marshal would get enough toughs together to kill him. Sure, he'd get a couple of them, but he'd be killed himself. And he had no quarrel with the marshal. The man wasn't the bravest in the world but, hell, he was trying to do what he had been hired to do. There were other places.

So on the sixth day, he saddled one of his horses, put a bedroll, a skillet, a coffeepot, and some groceries on the other, and rode north. He'd heard there were plenty of horse races at Albuquerque, and the horse he was riding was a damned good quarter-miler.

Seven

Hoeing weeds, wiping sweat from his eyes with a blue cotton bandana, Ace was thinking about how he'd never killed a lawman. Leaving El Paso had been the smart thing to do. Marshal Duggan was gone now and maybe he could go back. If not to El Paso, perhaps to Albuquerque. Or, he'd heard about Phoenix. Phoenix was a sporting town. But when he thought about the hanging of his brother and the Stockwell County sheriff, he swore under his breath. So he'd never shot a law dog. There was a first time for everything.

And when he looked up he saw the sheriff coming.

His hand went automatically to the .38, but he had no chance of surviving a shoot-out. No chance at all. The sheriff was surrounded by four men, all horseback, all armed with pistols and rifles. Ace was afoot. It would take too long to catch and saddle his horse. All he could do was lean on his hoe and watch them come, their horses trampling down cornstalks and stomping through the potato field.

The rider with a star on his shirtfront bellowed, "Throw up your hands, Bailey. We know who you are."

Ace continued leaning on his hoe, a half smile on his face.

"Do it, by God, or we'll make a sieve out of you." All five men had guns in their hands.

"I take it," Bailey drawled, "that you are Sheriff Cecil Petersen. Just happens I want a palaver with you."

50

"Unbuckle that gunbelt and let it drop. One wrong move and you'll be dead in a second."

Using his left hand, Ace unbuckled the belt and let the gun and holster drop in the dirt. One of the riders dismounted and picked it up.

"Get down on the ground. Face down." Sheriff Petersen was a lean, hard-looking man with high cheeks and a wide thin-lipped mouth under a long down-turned moustache. His eyes were squinty and cold.

By now, Mama Bailey had come out of the house, and the Reverend Bailey was hurrying toward them from the far side of the cornfield. "Does he get a trial?" Mama Bailey asked, trying to control the fear she felt. "Ever'one's s'posed to get a trial."

"Why, shore," one of the gunmen said. "We'll hang 'im the legal way."

"Just like you did my brother," Ace said, no longer smiling.

The elder Bailey was panting from hurrying. He said, "He's entitled to be tried by his peers. That means folks in this county. You hang him the way you did Jim, and you'll have the whole county after you."

"He'll get a trial," the sheriff said. "But if he's found innocent here, there's other sheriffs that want 'im. He's gonna get hung or spend a lot of years in prison. One or the other."

"Let's go," Ace said, walking toward the road.

"Halt. Stop right now or you're dead."

Ace stopped.

"Like I said, lay down on the ground, on your belly."

"Why should he have to do that?" Mama Bailey protested.

" 'Cause I said so. I ain't taking no chance of him runnin'." To Ace, Sheriff Petersen said, "You gonna lay down or am I gonna shoot you down?"

Papa Bailey protested, too. "You lawmen just like to

humiliate everybody. There's no need to treat him that way."

"Shut up or I'll arrest you for interferin' with the law."

Ace didn't say anything, but his eyes were fixed on the sheriff's face. In his mind, he vowed, you as much as touch my dad and I'll kill you. Somehow I'll put a bullet in your gut and watch you die.

"I'm gonna tell you one more time: Lay down."

Sure, Ace told himself, I'll do what I have to to survive, but I'm gonna live long enough to kill you, you sonofabitch. Moving slowly, he dropped to his knees, then stretched out on his stomach.

Sheriff Petersen got off his horse, pulled a pair of handcuffs from a back pocket, and twisted Ace's arms behind his back. When the cuffs were in place, he stepped aside. "Get up."

They made him walk the four miles to town with a rope around his neck and his hands shackled behind his back. In town, people stopped what they were doing and stared at the procession going down the hard-packed dirt street. They followed and asked, "Is that Ace Bailey? What're you gonna do with him, Sheriff?"

Sheriff Cecil Petersen was a proud man. "Yessir, this is him. He ain't so dangerous now. We're gonna treat him the way we treat all killers." He purposely made Ace walk the length of the main street, then double back to the sheriff's office and jail.

"You gonna hang 'im, Sheriff?"

"That'll be up to the judge. He'll get a fair trial."

"He ain't done nothin' so bad. Not around here, anyways."

"He's wanted all over the territory and half of Texas. I'm the one that captured him."

Ace was locked inside the one-cell jail behind the sheriff's office. The connecting door between the office and the jail was left open. Townspeople gathered outside, curious. Word spread. People came from forty miles away, hoping to get a look at the notorious killer. The sheriff allowed no one inside. No one, that is, except a newspaper reporter from Las Vegas who showed up two days later with a big awkward camera and a tripod.

"Folks in Las Vegas would like to see a picture of him in the newspaper. He's wanted for killing a man down there."

"Well, all right," Sheriff Petersen said. "I'll bring him outside for a minute so you can take a picture, but only for a minute."

A crowd gathered when Bailey was brought out in front of the sheriff's office. His hands were shackled in front now, but he was surrounded by deputies with six-guns in their hands.

"What's that feller gonna do?" a man asked. "Take a pitcher?"

"Yep. Now, you folks keep back. Stay away from him."

The reporter set up his camera on its tripod, put his head under a black cloth, and looked through the lens. He raised his head, picked up his equipment, and moved two steps closer. Bailey watched it all silently, a half smile on his face.

"Hey, Ace," a man yelled, "think you're gonna hang?"

Ace didn't answer. He didn't say anything.

"Oh, he's so handsome."

Bailey's eyes picked out the woman who had spoken. She was young, wearing a red bandana over her dark hair. He smiled.

Suddenly, the young woman rushed to him, wrapped her arms around his neck, and kissed him full on the mouth. Two pairs of hands pulled her away. "I just had to," she said breathlessly. "He's so handsome. I just had to touch him."

53

"Thank you kindly, miss," Ace said, smiling.

"Now, you folks stay back. I don't want no one to get close to him."

In spite of the sheriff's orders, the crowd moved nearer. "Can I kiss 'im too?" a woman asked. "Hey, Ace, I seen you eliminate them three J galoots. I'm gonna testify for you."

"Ain't he handsome? And so young."

"Get back now. Stay back." To the reporter, the sheriff said, "Come on, get your picture box ready."

"One moment. Okay. Now. I'm almost ready."

Sheriff Petersen stood close to Bailey, putting himself in the picture.

"Are you ready, Sheriff? Stand still now." A flash of black powder and the picture was taken.

"Are you gonna put that pitcher in the newspaper?" a man asked.

"Yessir," the reporter said. "We've got an engraver and everything."

The sheriff said, "Be sure you spell my name P—e—t—e—r—s—e—n. Not s—o—n."

"Yessir."

Back inside, the sheriff had two deputies point their guns at Bailey while the handcuffs were removed. With a sneer, the sheriff said, "Get in your cage, Mr. Ace Bailey. You're damned lucky you're alive. Most killers like you are hung without a trial." He gave Bailey a hard shove through the cell door and slammed it shut.

Ace kept his balance. And his smile. "I'm wondering, Mr. High Sheriff, how hard you tried to keep my brother from a mob, and I'm betting some of the mob are on your payroll. And while I'm wondering about that, I wonder how you're paying all these big brave deputies? Stockwell County ain't got that much money."

"That's none of your business." Suddenly, Sheriff Petersen let out a guffaw. "Hell, you ain't got no business."

Then just as suddenly, he turned serious. "I'll tell you something, killer: You might get a trial and these dumb shits might find you not guilty, but you ain't leaving this county alive. Get it? You're dead."

Ace's smile didn't slip. "How are you gonna arrange that, Mr. High Sheriff? Get your hired goons to bust in here and hang me?"

"There's ways." The guffaw returned. "Hell, you might try to bust out and get yourself shot. Haw-haw. There's lots of ways."

They fed Ace two meals a day and the food was barely edible. He didn't complain, but the sheriff expected him to. "Eat what you're given, killer. I don't care if you starve. Shit, the more you eat the more you shit, and the more you shit the more shit we have to carry out. Starve, you son of a bitch."

Every time Ace's folks came to visit, a deputy stood between them and the cell door, to be sure nothing was slipped through the bars. This time it was the deputy named Wylie.

"God be with you, Alvin," his mother said.

"We're praying for you," the Reverend Bailey said.

"Aw shit," the deputy said, a sneer in his voice. "All the prayin' in the world ain't gonna save his life."

"It might save his soul," Mama Bailey said.

"Shit."

"I'll thank you not to use vulgar language in front of my wife."

"Haw, I'll use whatever language I want. This ain't no goddamn church." The deputy was a big man, wide across the shoulders, with a short, thick neck and a flattened nose. He was a pug through and through. "Matter of fact, you been here long enough. Git."

"We're not through visiting," Mama Bailey said, "Give us another minute."

"I said git." The deputy grabbed Mrs. Bailey by the

55

shoulders, spun her around, and gave her a push.

"Here, now, stop that."

The senior Bailey's outrage was ignored. "You wanta be kicked out?"

"I'm going to mention this in my sermon. The county isn't going to like this."

"Shit on the goddamn county. Get your asses out of here."

Ace could do nothing. But he fixed the deputy's face in his mind and made another silent vow.

Pete Wylie is your name. Your death is my game.

Eight

They had to wait another week for the circuit judge to come around. The prosecuting attorney had traveled to Stockwell by stage from Raton and asked questions of the sheriff, then decided he had no real reason to charge Ace Bailey with murder. Manslaughter, maybe, but not murder. Not in Stockwell county, anyway. He understood, the attorney said, that Las Vegas had a better case against him. And he could be turned over to a U.S. Marshal and taken to Texas, where there was enough evidence to either hang him or send him to prison for a long time.

"I want 'im tried right here and sentenced right here," the sheriff said. "If all you can stick 'im with is manslaughter, then stick 'im with manslaughter. Them other sheriffs can wait. I'm the one that captured 'im."

"Very well. When the judge gets here, a trial date will be set."

"He's one dangerous hombre," Sheriff Petersen said. "If he gets half a chance, he'll run for it and we'll have to shoot 'im."

It was the next night that one of Stockwell's biggest sporting events took place. Ace was lying on the steel bunk, his hands under his head, gazing at nothing, when male voices brought him upright. He watched as a group of men, one by one, glanced up and down the street, then slipped through the door of the sheriff's office. One man let out a drunken titter and was immediately shushed by the others.

Soon some twenty men were on the jail side of the connecting door. The door was shut. They all looked with interest at Ace Bailey in the jail cell. "Hell, he ain't nothin' but a kid," one man said.

"Kid, hell. He's killed at least twenty men."

Among the mob was the big deputy named Pete Wylie. He began taking off his shirt.

Ace kept quiet, watching, hearing what they said but not understanding what they had in mind. He heard nothing about a hanging. There was no rope. He tried to figure out what to do if they opened the cell door and poured in after him. No way could he fight off that many men, but maybe he could grab a gun out of a holster and get a couple of them. Pete Wylie would be his first target. If he could kill that sonofabitch, his own death wouldn't be so bad. But still there was no talk of a hanging.

"I'm givin' two to one," a man said, waving a handful of greenbacks.

"Nosir," another said. "Make it four to one and I'll put up ten U.S. dollars."

"Okay, five'll get you twenty. Come one, come all."

By now Deputy Wylie had his shirt off. He was big. Broad muscles bulged in his shoulders and arms. He flexed his muscles, doubled his fists, and allowed, "Make it ten to one and you'll come out winner."

"I ain't bettin', but I wanta see the fun," a man said.

Money changed hands.

"Now listen," Deputy Wylie said. "Nobody outside this room is to know about this, savvy? The sheriff don't care, but nobody else is gonna know."

"Sure, Pete."

"Think he'll put up much of a fight, Pete?"

Ace knew then. Fear knotted his stomach, but he fought it down, trying to keep calm. Without speaking a word he stood, swung his arms to get the blood circulating, and waited. The cell door was opened, Wylie

58

slipped in, and the door was shut and locked.

"Hell, I'll bet he won't even try to fight."

"Bet ten he does. He's Ace Bailey. He'll try."

"Bet he won't last a minute."

"Even money?"

"Even money. Here's twenty. All or part of it."

"I'll take some of that."

"I got another twenty. That kid ain't worth a shit without a gun."

"Naw, he's a gunslinger not a fist fighter. I'll take odds he won't last thirty seconds."

"Hey, Pete, how long you think it'll take?"

"Twenty seconds," Pete said, flexing his shoulder muscles. He looked to be as big as a bull. "Not one second more."

"You gotta whup 'im 'til he cain't get up."

"Shit, gimme two to one and I'll bet he don't last fifteen seconds."

"Who's got a watch with a second hand on it?"

"I got one. Tell me when you're gonna start, Pete."

They were right, and Ace knew it. The deputy outweighed him by a good fifty pounds and was a saloon brawler. Ace was only a slender fellow of average height. He'd been in a few fist fights with his older brother and some of the neighboring boys as a kid, and there were some bloody noses and black eyes, but no one really hurt anyone. Maybe the smart thing to do was to just take his beating without resistance and get it over with. Maybe if he did, he'd live through the night. Yeah, just give up. Spoil their fun.

Like hell.

"Starting now," Wylie said.

The big deputy doubled his fists, held them in front of his face like a boxer, and shuffled toward Ace. Still silent, Ace doubled his fists and held them in front of his face. He waited.

The nose. That's where it would hurt the most. Smack

59

him on the nose. Make him bleed. Ace waited. The deputy shuffled closer.

Instead of backing away as the deputy expected, Bailey suddenly sprung forward, swinging his left fist then his right. His sudden move caught the big deputy by surprise. Ace felt the shock clear up to his shoulder as his right fist connected. It felt good.

Blood spurted from the deputy's nose.

Men shouted, cheered, stomped their feet. "Hey. Atta boy. He's gonna last a minute after all."

"Who's bettin' on thirty seconds? Here's ten."

"I'll cover your ten."

"He's a scrapper. I knew he'd fight."

But there would be no more surprises. Ace knew it. Deputy Wylie knew it.

Wiping his nose with his left arm, Wylie bored in, swinging his big fists wildly. Ace tried to see through the punches, see a chance to land one of his own. Big fists were coming at him too fast. A hard right hand caught him on the side of the head and he went numb. A mission bell started ringing in his ears. Blinking, he ducked, trying to get under the big man's arms. Then he saw an opening.

Ace bobbed up and butted the deputy in the face, staggering him. Then he swung both fists at the big middle. He heard a grunt, and kept swinging. Kept punching. Something hit him in the left eye. He felt no pain, only numbness, but his eye wouldn't open. He ducked again, and another blow caught him on top of the head.

The splintery wooden floor came up to meet him.

Vaguely, through the ringing in his ears, he could hear men yelling. One of them shouted, "Get up. Get up, goddamn it."

Sure. Get up. Get up and get knocked down again. Get up, hell.

Slowly, Ace got to his knees, then stood, feeling unsteady. Instinctively, he ducked again as the big deputy

60

swarmed over him. With his head in the man's belly, he drove with his legs and shoved him back against the cell door. Again he butted with his head.

"Atta boy, atta boy. Butt 'im again."

"He's a goddamn billy goat."

"Stay in there, kid."

"Thirty seconds. Thirty seconds is up."

"Goddamn it, Pete. Knock the hound dog shit out of 'im."

"You just lost me some money, Pete."

"Finish it, Pete."

A flurry of blows came Ace's way. He was forced to backpedal, and he fended off most of the blows by wrapping his arms around his face. And when the flurry let up a second, he saw an opening and swung his right fist. Felt it smack into the deputy's mouth.

"Hey, how about that? He ain't givin' up. Keep at it, kid."

"Shit, Pete, I thought you knew how to fight."

Growling with fury now, Pete bored in. A big fist crashed into the left side of Bailey's jaw. Another smacked against his forehead. His knees buckled, and he went down.

"Aw, goddamn it. Get up, kid."

"Finish 'im Pete."

Only half conscious now, Bailey got to his feet. His vision was blurred, and he could see only a vague shape in front of him. He managed to swing his fists, but he missed. Instead of a bell ringing in his ears, he could hear only a faint buzzing. Men were yelling, screaming with excitement, but he didn't hear. Two blows landed in his face.

The floor came up again.

"That's all," a man yelled. "He can't get up again."

"A fiver says he will."

"I'll call."

"It's payoff time, boys. He's done."

61

Ace Bailey heard none of that. What he heard were two voices competing with each other in his mind. One told him to stay down where he wouldn't be hit again. The other told him to get up. The voices were in his head, trying to outshout one another over the buzzing in his ears. Get up. Stay down, you fool. Get up and show the goddamn world you don't have to have a gun to fight.

"Come on, Ace," a man yelled. "I got a fiver on you."

Summoning all his strength, Ace got to his hands and knees. He shook his head, trying to clear his vision.

"A minute. A minute is up."

"He ain't up. You can't call it a minute 'til he's on his feet."

"Finish 'im, Pete. Goddamn it, kill the sonofabitch."

Ace stood, staggered two steps, then fell onto his hands and knees again.

"That don't count. He's got to stand up longer 'n that."

"Get up, Ace, goddamn it."

He stood again, weaving drunkenly. He saw the big shape come toward him. Ace swung his right fist. But it was too heavy, too slow.

A sharp pain and a bright light flashed through his brain at the same instant. He fell back, and his head hit the floor with a crack. He rolled onto his side, but darkness closed around him. He moved no more.

Nine

What passed for a courtroom in Stockwell County was a long one-room building built with green lumber. The lumber had shrunk and warped, leaving cracks in the walls and the floor. At one end was a platform raised a foot above the rest of the floor. A rough-sawed table served as the judge's bench. There was no jury box, and two plank benches had been placed in front of the platform for the jury. A wooden chair had been placed beside the judge's bench for a witness stand. Four rows of planks layed across sections of tree trunks were there for the spectators.

And the spectators gathered from fifty miles around. It was to be the first trial ever held in Stockwell County.

The crowd surged forward when Ace Bailey was brought out of the jail and walked down a dirt street to the courtroom. He had a deputy on each side of him and another behind him, all carrying drawn six-guns. Sheriff Cecil Petersen lead the procession, strutting, chest thrust out in front, ass thrust out in back, hat cocked on one side of his head.

"That's him. That's Ace Bailey."

"What happened to his face? He's all beat up."

"Nothin' serious," Sheriff Petersen said. "He tried to escape by slugging one of my deputies and he got the worst of the fight."

"He's not much more than a kid."

"Oh, the poor boy."

"Let me touch 'im. Just let me touch 'im, Mr. Sheriff."

"Keep back, now. Don't get close to him."

Bailey was silent, a half smile on his face. One eye was nearly closed, his upper lip was split, and his jaw was sore. But he considered himself lucky. He could have lost some teeth. He could have been stomped to death.

"Who beat 'im up?"

"Now, that's none of your concern. I promised I'd bring 'im to trial and that's what I'm doin'."

"The poor dear. Just let me touch 'im." The speaker was a young woman with brown hair to her shoulders, a pert round face, and a grey dress that came to her toes. She suddenly squeezed through the crowd and wrapped her arms around Bailey's neck.

The crowd cheered. "That's the way, Mabel. Kiss 'im again."

It took two deputies to pull her away.

"Thank you kindly, ma'am."

"I'm on your side, Ace. I'm gonna testify for you."

"Keep back, now. Stay away from him."

Judge Frederic Freytag had a half-dozen towns in his district, and he didn't believe in spending much time in any of them. But this was an important trial. Newspaper reporters were here from Santa Fe, Albuquerque, Raton, and Las Vegas. As the presiding judge, his name would be in the newspapers.

"Mr. Bailey," the judge said, looking down from his bench at the defendant standing handcuffed before him, "you are charged with the deaths of Mr Jasper Short, Mr. Jason Hammer, and Mr. James Wilheim."

"Yeah," a spectator shouted. "That's them. Was them. Haw-haw."

"Silence." The judge pounded the plank with his gavel.

The courtroom was filled to overflowing. Spectators outside peered through the cracks in the walls to see what was happening. Nearly all carried six-guns. The chosen jurors all carried six-guns too, and even the judge had a gun out of sight behind the bench. By late afternoon, the trial was under way. A lawyer from Raton had been hired by the Reverend and Mrs. Bailey to represent their son. The Baileys had done all the work finding witnesses.

First in the witness chair was a hunchedbacked little man who worked in the mercantile. He testified that he had seen the shooting. Two of the three J's, he said, had been poking fun at Preacher Bailey, but they meant no harm. The other wasn't even there.

"Are you saying," the prosecutor asked, "that one of the three, a Mr. James Wilheim, was shot down in cold blood?"

"I reckon."

Outside, men jostled one another to get an eye to the cracks in the walls. "What'd he say? What's goin' on in there?"

A bearded spectator turned his head away from a crack long enough to reply, "He said he seen it all. He said them three was only funnin'."

"I seen it, too. I'm gonna testify."

Judge Freytag's stomach told him it was supper time. He was looking forward to having his nightly glass of whiskey, a comfortable bed in the Stockwell Hotel, and a good book. Besides, the wooden chair he was sitting on was getting damned uncomfortable. He pounded the plank with his gavel. "This court is recessed until tomorrow morning at eight o'clock. Make that eight-thirty."

Again a crowd followed Bailey and his escorts back to the jail. But this time they kept their distance.

Locked in his cell, Ace said nothing when Sheriff Petersen taunted him. "No matter how this trial turns out, you're a dead man, Bailey. You'd better get your preacher pa to pray all night for you, 'cause you've got no more than a few days to live."

As before, half of Stockwell County gathered the next morning when Ace Bailey was led outside. He blinked in the early morning sunlight and studied the faces around him. There were his mother and dad and a few neighbors he remembered from his childhood. And there was another familiar face. It was a man's face with a long-handled grey moustache. The man wore a big dirty white stetson and had a star pinned to his left shirt pocket. Ace recognized him as the sheriff from Las Vegas. Even if he won this trial, he wouldn't be free. That lawman no doubt had another warrant for his arrest.

Before noon, the prosecution rested its case. Two more witnesses said Bailey had shot James Wilheim in the back as he was running away. The prosecutor believed he had built a good enough case to get a conviction of manslaughter if not murder.

The first witness for the defense wanted to tell the jurors and every one else within hearing distance what kind of men the three J's were, but the prosecutor objected.

"It's immaterial, Your Honor. All we should concern ourselves with is what happened at that particular time on that particular day." The judge sustained the objection.

"But," said the witness, a lean-jawed man in bib overalls, "I just wanta say —"

Bang went the gavel.

It made no difference. Everyone knew what the witness wanted to say.

At the end of the day, the prosecutor wasn't so sure. Witnesses saw two of the J's shoot at Preacher Bailey's feet. "That kid," one of them said, "was just standin' there mindin' his own business until he saw his pa was bein' shot at. Sure, ol' Wilheim wasn't doin' any of the shootin', but he was one of the three that'd stole, killed, and bullied for years in Stockwell County."

66

The prosecutor asked the judge to order the jury to ignore that last remark, and the judge did. But he wasted his breath. The jury wasn't going to be told what to consider and what not to consider.

The trial would go to the jury before noon the next day, then Judge Freytag and the prosecuting attorney could ride the stage back to Raton, a town with a railroad and more comfortable accommodations. The judge made sure the newspaper reporters got his name spelled correctly, but the prosecutor tried to stay away from them. He didn't much want his name connected with a verdict of not guilty. If by some quirk he won his case, then that would be the time to make a grand speech to the press.

When the handcuffs were removed and Ace Bailey was again shoved roughly into his cell, the taunts resumed. "You think it's going your way, don't you, shithead? You might not even live to hear the verdict. We can shoot you right now and drag your carcass outside. We got a right to shoot a prisoner that tries to run for it."

Supper was barely edible and chewing with a sore jaw was painful, but Ace forced it down. He needed his strength. Any minute now they could come for him—probably that big deputy—shoot him, and say it was self-defense. All he could hope for was that they'd open the cell door first, give him at least a small chance. But they wouldn't. They could stand outside and shoot between the bars. Any time now.

Ace believed he was facing death. It didn't scare him. He'd worked hard most of his life, but he'd lived darned well at times, too. And everyone had to die. Every creature God made had to die. Death was just the end of living. That's all. Just the end.

Yeah, he said to himself, when I'm dead I'm dead. Any time now.

But daylight came with nothing happening. Probably,

he thought, because they could keep him here at least one more night no matter what the verdict was. That law dog from Las Vegas wouldn't start out with him until the next day. It was a long way to Las Vegas. Maybe he'd have a chance to escape.

Naw. Sheriff Petersen would see that he didn't live beyond tonight.

The crowd was there when Ace Bailey was again marched from the jail to the courtroom. They surrounded the prisoner and the deputies, but obeyed Sheriff Petersen's orders to stay back. One more witness testified that Preacher Bailey and Mrs. Bailey were being rawhided and shot at that day by Jasper Short and Jason Hammer. He admitted, under cross-examination, that James Wilheim hadn't been doing any of the rawhiding, but added that if he'd lived he would have been a threat to the Baileys. The judge ordered the jurors to ignore that last remark. He suspected they wouldn't.

Both sides rested and delivered their final arguments. The killing was purely in defense of his parents, Bailey's lawyer said. Shooting a man in the back could be nothing but cold-blooded murder, the prosecutor said. The judge, in his instructions to the jurors, gave them three choices: murder, manslaughter, or innocent. If they found that James Wilheim had not been a threat to anyone at that particular time and was shot in the back, then they had to find the defendant guilty of murder or manslaughter, he said.

The room was cleared while the jury deliberated. It took less than an hour.

Not guilty.

A loud cheer went up from the spectators inside the room. Folks outside shouted, "What'd they say? What'd they say?"

"Not guilty. They said he's not guilty."

More cheering.

When Bailey was led outside, the people again surrounded him and the deputies. "What's he in handcuffs for, Sheriff? He's not guilty."

Sheriff Petersen growled, "Yeah, but there's other jurisdictions that've got warrants for his arrest. Sheriff Ackley from Las Vegas is here with a warrant. I'm turnin' this prisoner over to him."

A disappointed groan rumbled through the crowd. One of the witnesses got between the deputies and patted Ace on the back. "We done the best we could, Ace."

Two deputies pushed him away.

While they were doing that, a woman slipped through. "Oh, the poor man. I just have to touch him." Instead of throwing her arms around Ace's neck, she grabbed him around the waist and hugged him, her body tight against his. Then she moved her hands down between them. He felt her hands groping for his shackled ones.

She whispered, "Here, take it. I'll meet you on the road west of town."

Ten

Ace Bailey slipped the gun, a small derringer, inside his shirt, between two buttons, then under the waistband of his pants. The woman kept her body tight against his until she was sure the gun was out of sight, then allowed herself to be pulled away.

Pure anguish showed in her face. "I love you, Ace. I'll always love you."

Surprise flashed into Ace Bailey's mind, but only for a moment. As a professional card player, he instantly controlled his expression and smiled a half smile. "Thank you kindly, ma'am."

While his mouth formed the words, his brain registered the fact: She had long chestnut hair and a pretty face. She was Marybelle Stewart, the woman he'd met on the prairie one night south of Raton.

He kept his shackled hands pressed against the gun. His biggest fear at the moment was that it would slip down and fall out his pants leg. With his hands against it, the slight bulge it made didn't show.

His worst moment came when the handcuffs were removed in the doorway of his cell. Instead of extending his hands while the shackles were unlocked, he kept them pressed against the gun. Immediately, when his hands were free, he turned around and walked into the cell. The door was slammed and locked. The deputies left.

Certain now that no one was in sight, he took the gun out and examined it. Just a little .22 single shot. A Remington, flat, designed to be carried in a vest pocket. But it was a weapon. Maybe it wouldn't save his life, but now he could get at least one of his would-be killers.

Supper was the usual cold fried potatoes, cold beef, and lukewarm coffee. They wouldn't trust him with a knife to cut the meat so he had to eat with his fingers. He forced down every scrap, then pushed the plate and fork under the cell door. Now it was waiting time.

How would they do it? Would they shoot him in the cell and carry his body outside? Would they come as a masked mob and hang him? Naw, they wouldn't hang him. The whole county suspected they'd hung an innocent man when they hung Jim Bailey. Another hanging like that would have the county ready to run the sheriff out of the territory. No, they'd have to make it look like an attempt to escape. Sure, when they came to pick up his supper plate, he'd jumped them and tried to wrestle a gun away from them. That's the way it would happen. They couldn't let a killer escape.

He waited. After making sure the little gun was loaded, he'd shifted it to his left side under his waistband and kept one button of his shirt opened. He practiced grabbing it. The gun had no trigger guard, and he had to be sure he didn't pull the trigger too soon.

She'd be on the road west of town, she'd said. How long would she be there? Would she have horses? Why did she want him out of jail?

He lay on the iron bunk and waited. It was quiet in the sheriff's office.

Darkness came. He couldn't see across the cell. They would have to bring a lantern. Ace Bailey forced himself to relax. He lay back with his hands under his head. Then the door between the sheriff's office and the jail opened.

The first thing Bailey saw was a lantern, then the big hulk of Deputy Wylie. The deputy closed the door and held the lantern up to the cell. "You in there, Bailey?

71

Haw-haw, sure you are." He put the lantern on the floor and lifted his six-gun out of its holster.

"You right with your maker, Bailey? If you ain't, that's tough tit."

He knew then how it was supposed to happen. Well, he'd make it easy. Bailey stood and stepped up to the cell bars, leaning against them. "What are you gonna do? Shoot between the bars?"

"Yup. Stand right there so you'll get powder burns on you. You tried to grab my gun when I came for your supper plate. I out-rassled you and you got shot. Haw."

Bailey had his thumbs hooked inside the waistband of his pants, his right hand near the derringer, The deputy brought the six-gun up, aimed at his heart. Close. The deputy's thumb started to cock the hammer back. Bailey's right hand darted inside his shirt. The derringer cracked.

Deputy Wylie's eyes crossed as a round hole appeared in his forehead. His knees buckled and he collapsed.

As he fell, Ace Bailey reached between the bars, grabbed his shirtfront, and held him close until he hit the floor. Then he grabbed the six-gun and prepared to shoot whoever came through the connecting door. No one came. Next he reached between the bars and lifted the jail key out of the dead man's hip pocket. Soon he was free.

He started to tiptoe to the connecting door, then realized that was useless. If anyone was there, they'd heard the shot. Ace walked in as if he belonged there, and he was surprised to find it empty. When he thought about it later, he figured out why. The sheriff and the other deputies were waiting where they would be seen, either at the cafe or at the saloon, leaving it up to Deputy Wylie to do the dirty work. That way, if anyone got suspicious, they could say they had nothing to do with it.

Bailey rummaged through the sheriff's desk until he located his pearl-handled .38 and its holster and belt. He buckled it on and found his black hat hanging from a peg. Outside, there were no street lights. The only light came from the window of the mercantile and the open door of the saloon. No use tiptoeing. He walked like a man going on about his business, but got around a corner and in an alley as soon as he could. Then he proceeded rapidly out of town.

While he walked he could only hope the woman would be waiting there somewhere. If she wasn't, what would he do? He couldn't go to his folks' farm. That was the first place the sheriff and his goons would look for him. Hell, he'd have to walk all the way to Uncle Amos's place, and that was a long way. And he'd have to stay out of sight of the road. Stay out of sight of everyone.

Just west of Stockwell was a low hill, low but long. He'd had too little to eat in the past ten days and was out of condition. Huffing, feeling a little weak in the knees, he kept his eyes moving, hoping to spot the woman. At the same time he cussed Sheriff Cecil Petersen for feeding him so little. At the top of the hill, he paused and looked back. The lights were barely visible. All was quiet. Then Ace realized he could be seen against the skylight, and he dropped to his haunches. But on second thought, he had to be seen. If she was there, she had to see him. He stood again.

"Hey," a woman's voice came out of the dark, "whoever you are, you've got a long way to walk."

Squinting, trying to see her, he answered, "Unless you're Marybelle Stewart, you're lost in the dark." The vague shape of two horses came out of the night, with the black range of mountains behind them. She was riding one and leading another.

She said, "If I didn't know Ace Bailey was in jail, I'd think you were him."

"I'm Ace."

"Want to ride or do you like to walk?"

Grinning in the dark, he answered, "Never walk when

you can ride, I always say."

"Take the reins and climb up on this pony. He's gentle."

As much by feel as by sight, he took the reins from her hand, found the stirrup on the left side of the horse, put his left foot in it, and swung into the saddle.

"Are you horseback?"

"Yup."

"Let's ride." She took off at a fast trot, going west. He followed. They rode at that gait for half an hour before she spoke again, "I knew they'd wait 'til dark to try to kill you. I wasn't sure you'd survive."

"How'd you know they were gonna try to kill me?"

"That sheriff has a mean eye. He was ready to chew horseshoes when the jury said you were innocent. And I heard about how they hung your brother. I figured you had only a short time to live."

"That little pistol saved my life. You saved my life. One of the deputies was going to shoot me in the jail cage."

"I'll bet it was the big one, the one named Wylie."

"He's the one. He's dead."

"Well, I won't grieve for him." She reined off the road then, heading southwest. The horses' hooves pounded the earth. Ace kept his mount even with hers.

"You act like you're going someplace." he said.

"Yup."

"Well, not that it's any of my business or anything, but would you mind telling me where?"

"Guess."

"Well, it ain't Raton, so it must be Albukirk or someplace in between."

"In between."

They rode silently for a while, then it came to him. "You wouldn't be heading for Eagle Nest Lake, would you?"

"Good guess."

74

"Uh-huh. And now I know why you helped me bust out of jail."

"You didn't think I wanted your young body, did you?"

"Those human bones must be awful important."

"They are. And it appears you're the only one who can find them."

"Yeah, I can find them."

"Will you do it?"

"I owe it to you."

About two hours before daylight, Ace said, "We'd better find a place to rest these ponies. Unless you want to be afoot."

"I could use some rest myself."

They kept going until the horses' backs dipped downhill, then leveled off again. "This might be the best spot," Ace said. "I think we're in a deep draw."

Working mostly by feel, they loosened the cinches, then hobbled the horses' forefeet. "I doubt that sheriff and his goons will be looking in this direction for a day or two. They'll think I headed for my folks' place, and they'll think my folks are hiding me."

"We're probably out of his jurisdiction, but he won't let a little thing like that stop him."

"Prob'ly not. Boy, it feels good to be out of that durned jail."

"I know the feeling."

Trying to see her face in the dark, he said, "You do? Come to think of it, you're no greenhorn."

"My dad . . . you know, I told you about him. Well, no, I didn't, did I? Well, he was an outlaw. He hated trains, and robbing them was his favorite pasttime."

Ace lay back on the ground, using his hat for a pillow. From the sound of rustling clothes and a small grunt, he guessed she had sat on the ground about ten feet away. "Why'd he hate trains?"

"They robbed him. At least that's the way he saw it. He was raising cattle—and me—in Colorado, north of

Colorado Springs, when a government honcho came along and told him he'd have to go. Seems the U.S. government gave that land to the railroad to help finance it. Dad . . . well, he tried to obey the law but he didn't know much about it, and somehow he hadn't filed a claim on the land."

"Uh-huh. So the railroad kicked him off."

"Yes. They had a bunch of toughs on their payroll to do just that."

"So your pop started robbing trains to get even."

"Yup."

"And he took you along?"

"At first. Mother died when I was three, and Dad had no place to leave me. I was fifteen when he robbed his first train. He put me on a horse and took me along. I held the horses. Over the next two years, I was on some long, fast horseback rides. Once, in Albuquerque, four of us were arrested. The authorities didn't know what else to do with me so they put me in a separate cell. Somebody smuggled a gun to my dad and he busted us all out. After that, Dad put me in a boarding school in Denver. He said he wanted me to be a lady."

"So that's how you know what it's like to be locked in a cage."

"Yup."

"Which brings up another question, one I've asked before. Why is it so important to find your pop's remains? And don't tell me you only want to give him a decent burial."

"You're asking too many questions."

"Yeah, I reckon I am. But if I'm gonna ride across country with you, I ought to know what for."

"Like you said, you owe it to me. I'm gonna try to sleep now."

"Yeah, I owe you."

She was quiet while Bailey mulled over everything

she'd said. Then he asked. "Money? Did he disappear with some loot from a robbery?"

"I'm not telling any more. All you have to do is show me those skeletons. Then we'll be even."

"Uh-huh. That's what it is, all right. Money."

Eleven

They stayed where they were until first light. Ace dozed once for a few minutes, and he guessed that she was asleep. When it was light enough, he saw her stretched out on her side, using a big black hat for a pillow as he had. She was dressed in the same slouchy overalls with a boy's lace-up shoes on her feet. Her long chestnut hair sprawled over her face. The two horses were grazing on good grass a hundred yards away. Both were bay geldings, one with a white spot between his eyes and a white stocking on his left hind leg. The other had no white at all. The saddles on their backs were old, close to being worn out but still usable. With their forefeet hobbled, they had to hop-step to move, and when they stepped on the bridle reins, it took them a few seconds to get free. They'd be easy to catch.

Standing and stretching, Ace climbed out of the draw they were in and looked back the way they'd come. No sign of anything alive; just jagged yucca, thorny cane cactus, and yellow sunflowers. Mount Capulin was north and a little west. The Raton Mountains were beyond that. High, steep mesas were all around them. He figured they were east and maybe a little north of Cimarron.

Shivering in the early morning cold, he glanced back at her and saw she hadn't moved. He took that opportunity to unbutton his pants and relieve himself. He wondered if she had any coffee in the saddlebags on the horse she had ridden. Not that it mattered. Smoke from a fire could be seen for five miles.

Sheriff Petersen and his hoodlum deputies would probably spend most of the day searching the Bailey farm. But Ace couldn't be sure about that. The faster they got into those Sangre de Cristos, the better.

Walking back to where she was lying, he said, "Hey, wake up."

"Huh?" Her eyes popped open and she sat up. "Brrr," She shivered, stood, and hugged herself. "My God. It's daylight."

"I'll go get the horses." Purposely, he stayed on the other side of the horses, out of her sight, hoping she would find enough privacy to drain her bladder. He took his time going back, leading the horses.

When she rummaged through the saddlebags, his only wish at the moment was that she would produce something to eat. She did. "There's bread and some cured ham here," she said, handing him a package wrapped in heavy paper.

"Boy, am I hungry." He unwrapped a loaf of bread and a five-pound ham. "I found my gun in the sheriff's desk, but not my pocket knife. Hope you've got one."

"Yes." She dug into the pockets of the baggy overalls. "Here."

He opened the longer of the two blades and sliced two pieces from the bread and the ham. "Breakfast is served."

"In a minute." She was rummaging through the saddlebags.

"Looking for coffee?" he asked.

"No, I'm looking for . . . here it is." She took a woman's dress from a saddlebag, then her long comb. The dress she carefully folded and put back, then began running the comb through her hair.

Grinning around a mouthful of bread, he said, "I know I look like something the cat dragged up, but I'd

79

rather eat than comb my hair."

"That's one of the differences between a man and a woman. I'll eat in a minute." Again he had to admire her face and slender figure. In spite of the touch of hardness around her eyes, she was well-groomed and pretty. He estimated her age at around thirty-five.

Before the sun came up they were riding at a steady trot, going west. She sat her saddle comfortably. Every time they crossed a low rise, Bailey dismounted, went back to the top, and studied the country behind them. He saw no one. About noon they crossed the railroad tracks that led to Santa Fe. In a draw out of sight of the tracks, they stopped, let the horses graze and rest, and ate more bread and ham.

Bailey tried again to find out why she wanted to go to the skeletons, but she refused to answer. "Well, at least tell me this much. Where did the robbery take place?"

"What robbery?"

"The one your pop pulled before he disappeared."

"You're only guessing."

"I'm guessing right, though, ain't I?"

"You don't need to know any more."

By mid afternoon, they crossed the old Santa Fe trail.

"We'll get to Cimarron soon after dark," Bailey said. "There's a building there that passes for a hotel and eating house. If you want to, you can prob'ly get a comfortable bed and a meal there. I'd better stay out of sight."

"I've been there before, you know. And I'll have to stop and buy some groceries, anyway."

"What're you using for money? Last time I saw you you had to have breakfast on me."

"There are ways."

"What ways? You didn't rob anybody, did you?"

"No, I'm no thief. That's all you need to know."

For some reason he wasn't sure of himself, he didn't tell Marybelle Stewart about his sister Mindy. His repu-

80

tation had gotten his brother hung, and that sheriff back in Stockwell County was probably giving his folks a hard time because of him. Leave Mindy out of it, he told himself. For all he knew, word had reached Cimarron that she was Ace Bailey's sister, and soon word would spread that he'd killed a deputy and busted out of jail. Any strangers seen in or around her house at night would be suspected. So it was another dark and cold camp for Ace Bailey.

They'd seen the lights of Cimarron after nightfall and had split up. Their plan was to meet next morning near the road out of town, the one leading to Cimarron Canyon. He'd stay out of sight of the road but would be where he could watch for her. He remembered the country east of Cimarron as good grass country, and when he got a hill between him and the town, he unsaddled and hobbled his horse.

"You'll get a better feed than I will, old boy," he said to the horse. "Wish I could eat buffalo grass. Wish I could see in the dark like you. Wish I could build a fire and warm up this ham and bread. Wish I had a can of beans. Wish . . . Aw hell, might as well wish in one hand and spit in the other, and see which gets full."

His cold meal chewed and swallowed, he wrapped himself in the short tarp the woman had carried behind her saddle, lay on his side, and drew his knees up, trying to keep warm. This running from the law was no way to live. A man could get enough of this in a hurry. What he'd like to do was to go back to El Paso, and if that turned out to be dangerous, then get farther away . . . Arizona, perhaps. Surely, nobody had heard of Ace Bailey that far west. If he could do that, he might quit carrying a gun and live a peaceable life. Peaceable and a hell of a lot more comfortable. He'd gamble only with gentlemen and stay away from the kind of men who started fights.

81

Then maybe in ten years or so he could come back to see his folks. And his sister. Goddamn, he swore under his breath, I'm only a few miles from Mindy and a good meal, and I don't dare be seen around there. Nosir, this ain't the way to live.

Eventually, weariness took over, and in spite of the chilly night air, Ace Bailey slept.

Just before daylight one of the Reverend Bailey's prayers was answered. It rained. "Goddamn," Ace Bailey said aloud. "Excuse me, Pop, but once in a while a man has to cuss." He wrapped the tarp around his shoulders while he ate the rest of the ham and bread. Then he caught and saddled the bay gelding. The horse didn't like the wet blanket and saddle any better than he did, and when Ace stepped into the saddle, it had a hump in its back. When he moved it out of its tracks, it crow-hopped a few jumps. "Don't blame you a-tall, old boy," Ace said. "If somebody put a cold, wet saddle on my back, I'd stick his head in the ground so far all you'd see of him would be his feet. You're better natured than I am."

The rain had turned into a drizzle by the time he came to the road on the north side of town. Ace turned back far enough to see the road in the distance, and he reckoned that if anyone saw him, they'd think he was a rancher or hired cowboy heading for town. He waited there in the drizzling rain for more than an hour. And when he saw her, he wasn't sure it was Marybelle. This rider was on a bay horse with one white stocking, and she or he had on a slouchy black hat. But the rider also had on a long yellow rain slicker.

"Goddamn," he muttered, "That could be anybody."

Then he saw the fat blanket roll behind the cantle and knew it was somebody going somewhere. And yeah, if she had enough money, she would have bought herself a slicker. He rode in her direction, cautiously at first, then at a trot.

She saw him coming, stopped her horse, and waited. I trust you had a good night's sleep," she said with a wry smile.

"Shore. You betcha. How about yourself?"

"In spite of my appearance, they treated me well. I bought two blankets. How about taking some of this load off my horse and putting it on yours."

As he transferred some of the bulky load from behind her cantle, he unwrapped a small coffeepot. "Now this," he said, "is just what the doctor ordered. That is, if you bought some coffee."

"Coffee, canned fruit, jerky, and a slab of bacon. But I'd like to get traveling before we stop to eat. Unless you're too weak from starvation to travel."

"Me? Why I just dined like a prince. Let's travel." Suddenly, he stopped what he was doing and gave her a hard stare. "Jerky? Did you say jerky?"

"Yup. What's wrong with jerky?"

"Nothing, if you've got jaws like a wolf."

"Aw, some folks simply don't know what to do with it." She got her horse moving again and he rode up beside her.

Five hours later he got his first hot meal in twelve days, under the high palisade cliffs of Cimarron Canyon. He found enough dead lower limbs on the pine trees to build a fire. While coffee boiled and bacon fried, the Cimarron River splashed and gurgled happily downstream. He asked, "Did you hear anything in Cimarron about me? Busting out of jail? Or anything?"

"I didn't. But then I probably wouldn't have. News of your jailbreak couldn't have reached there yet."

Drizzling rain caused the fire to sputter, but it put out enough heat to curl the bacon strips. They took turns drinking scalding black coffee out of the one tin cup she had. They ate the bacon with their fingers. "Boy," he said, "that was good. You'd do to camp with."

"I've done this before, you know."

"I can tell. I can tell, too, that you've got an education. Was it that boarding school in Denver?"

"Yes sir. And you? You speak well for a drifting gunhand."

"My pop has a good education. He's a preacher, you know, and he knows his grammar. He tried to teach it to his young'uns. My mom, now, she was raised in the Ozarks of Missouri, and she talks like it. But she's a good soul." A worry wrinkle suddenly appeared on Bailey's forehead. He swallowed hard and was silent a moment.

She said, "You're worried about your folks, aren't you? That sheriff strikes me as being a bullying brute."

A little grey dipper flew from rock to rock in the river, now and then ducking into the water for food. Barely audibly, Bailey muttered, "Cecil Petersen don't know it yet, but he's dead."

"You're going to kill again, then." It was an accusation.

Remembering the thoughts that had run through his head the night before, he said, still barely audibly, "Seems like the world won't let a man quit."

Twelve

They were out of the canyon and had started the long climb over the divide to Eagle Nest Lake when they decided to camp for the night. More coffee, bacon, and bread had him feeling better, stronger. The meal over, they took turns sipping the remainder of the hot coffee. The rain had stopped and stars sparkled all over the sky.

"You're sure you can find that knoll?"

"Yup. I might not go directly to it, but I'll find it."

"I wish I'd had enough money to buy a packhorse. I might need one."

"The loot must be in gold, then."

She was silent a moment, then said, "You're guessing again."

"Naw. I don't have to guess. Nothing else makes sense."

"You think you're smart."

"Naw. It doesn't take much smarts. Your dad and his partners pulled a robbery, then disappeared. You looked for them in every city and decided they'd stayed away from the cities. So you started combing the hills. Only thing I can't figure out is why it took you so long."

"You don't know everything after all."

"Nope. I never claimed to know everything. I never know as much as I ought to."

"Good night." She wrapped herself in a blanket and her long yellow slicker and stretched out on the ground.

"Good night? That's all?"

Her voice was muffled by the blanket. "I hope you aren't so foolish as to get romantic notions."

Not knowing what to say to that, he said nothing more that night.

It was a long, hard climb to the top of the divide, made worse by having to get off the road twice and hide when they saw wagons coming down. In some places they followed old trails instead of the road and had to traverse the hills. The sun was out and after the rain the land was green with lush high-country grass. Wildflowers of every color dotted the hills and meadows. A herd of deer grazing on a hillside merely raised their heads and watched them.

About noon they stopped, rested the horses, and ate a cold meal. Ace tried to pump more information out of Marybelle about what she hoped to find, but he got nowhere. Late in the afternoon they topped the divide and looked down on the handful of buildings called Eagle Nest. She said, "Can we get there yet tonight?"

"No. It'll take another five or six hours." Nodding toward a stand of tall pines, he said, "Let's get on the other side of those trees. See if we can find a creek and make camp."

That evening he learned how to make chili con carne with beef jerky. Fascinated, he watched as she dipped water from a narrow stream into a small iron pot, putting in some of the jerky, a handful of red chili, and a double handful of cornmeal. She pounded it all into a mixture, put it in the fire, and added water twice as it boiled. They ate out of the pot. It wasn't bad.

"You call it jerky," she said by way of conversation. "Mexicans call it *carne seco*. Give a Mexican ten pounds of *carne seco*, a cone of *penoche*—brown sugar, that is—and a serape, and he can walk two hundred miles across the mountains."

"I wouldn't be surprised. I tried to live with some

86

Mexicans once and had to give up. Their cooking tasted good, but it gave me the . . ." Not wanting to explain further, he let his voice trail off.

"I know. I tried it, too. Only the Mexicans and Indians can live the way they do."

"I've never had any quarrel with the Mexicans. An Indian, now, I wouldn't trust. But I always got along with the Mexicans."

After a few moments of silence, he changed the subject. "I'm afraid you're gonna be disappointed. I walked around on that knoll quite a while and I didn't see any money."

"Did you look for anything in particular?"

"No."

"Then you could have overlooked it."

"It has to be loot from a robbery. They were prob'ly headed for Albukirk and were taking a long way around to try to fool the laws. That's why they were caught far from the wagon road. The robbery took place in either Trinidad or Raton. Prob'ly Raton. If they'd robbed something in Trinidad, they'd have had to come over the Raton Pass, and that would be a good place to get caught."

"Not necessarily. There are other ways over the Raton Mountains. Ever hear of the Trinchera Pass? You can't get a wagon over it, but it's easy enough for horsebackers. And over west a dozen miles or so there's another horseback pass."

"Yeah, but there's a telegraph in Trinidad and Raton. Every place they could come out of those mountains, the laws would have been waiting for them. No, it happened in Raton."

Shrugging her shoulders, she said, "It doesn't matter now, does it?"

"Naw. They got away from the laws, then got killed by some Indians."

"Good night."

"You're sure turning in early."

"There's nothing else to do." Her voice had a final ring to it. "And I mean nothing."

"Yeah, yeah."

They rode south, staying west of the wagon road. They rode silently until Ace commented, "These old ponies are glad to be going downhill for a change. They need a rest."

"How much farther?"

"Not much. Where'd you get these horses?"

"I borrowed one and bought the other, the one you're riding."

"Borrowed? Who from?"

"A friend. Never mind who."

"If you want my help, you ain't gonna be able to keep all these secrets."

"Show me where those remains are and leave. I won't need your help any longer."

"Yeah, yeah."

They turned west, and Bailey said, "A couple of miles. When we get on the other side of those quakers and pines, we ought to see the hill."

But he was wrong. The country before them dipped into a narrow valley and slanted up to a rocky ridge covered with huge boulders. "Well, we'll have to go farther south," Bailey said. Mountain grasses were stirrup high, and he mused, "Good cattle country in the summer. Sure would hate to spend the winter here, though." She was silent, and he added, "A feller could get snowbound up here and stuck 'til May. Or June."

Thirty minutes later they rode out of a stand of tall timber, and he reined up. "That's it. Yonder. See it?"

"Yes. It is a knoll, just as you described it."

"Yup. If I had a bunch of Indians on my trail, and I had to take a stand and make a fight of it, there's where I'd head for."

It was noon when they reached it. He stayed on his horse a few minutes while she walked slowly and carefully among the skeletal remains of humans and horses. Bits of clothing and parched skin clung to the skeletons. Every time she found a skull in the tall grass, she gasped, "Oh. Oh, my God." The skulls seemed to grin an evil grin at being disturbed. Bailey dismounted finally, but he stayed with his horse and remained silent.

"O-o-h, my. My God." She picked up a saddle with dried and curled leather skirts, then carefully put it back on the ground where she'd found it. Next she picked up the remains of a boot, but immediately dropped it and jumped back as foot bones fell out. "O-o-h." Looking at Bailey with clouded eyes, she said, "It has been only six years. How could everything deteriorate so fast?"

He started to say something about coyotes, wolves, and magpies, but instead he said. "Any idea which one was your pop?"

"No . . . uh . . . I don't know." Over and over, she exclaimed, "O-o-h. O-o-h, my God." Finally, with a mixture of distaste and anxiety on her face, she looked up at Bailey. "Are you sure it was Indians who did this?"

"Like you said, I'm only guessing. But there's the bones of four men and two horses. I don't know how many horses they had, but some of them survived the fight and were stolen by whoever attacked. And I don't see any guns. Indians can't get enough horses and guns."

"It could have been white men."

"Yeah, it could have. But this is a good place to fort up, and whoever attacked these four had them outnumbered by . . . I'd reckon at least five to one. That means either Indians or the U.S. Army. I'd bet on Indians."

"There must have been some dead and wounded on the other side."

"No doubt about that. Those empty shell casings tell me the fight lasted a while. With that many shots fired and with the Indians in open country, there had to have

89

been some dead ones. Indians try to carry their dead away."

"But Indians wouldn't have any use for . . ." She shut her mouth when she realized what she was about to say.

"Gold? No, Not renegade Indians. But they'd know what it was and they'd prob'ly take it anyway."

"Well." She looked down at her laced shoes a moment, then back at him. "You can go on about your business now."

"What business?"

"I don't know. Whatever you'd do if you'd got out of jail by yourself."

"I'm sure curious about what you expect to find here."

"It's none of your business."

"If we had a shovel, we could bury those . . . uh . . . those remains."

"That's not your concern either."

"If it's paper money, it's rotted by now. If it's gold, it can't be hard to find. I don't see any shovel. If they'd had a shovel to bury the loot with, we'd find at least part of the shovel."

"You can keep the horse you're riding. I paid for him. And you can take some of the groceries."

"You want to stay here by yourself?"

"I've camped by myself before."

"There's a store down at that little settlement called Angel. If you've got any money left, you can buy a shovel."

"Go. Get."

"First time I saw you, you had a rifle. You ain't got a gun of any kind now. What happened to it?"

"I sold it. Not that it's any of your business."

"First time I saw you, you were out of groceries. Where'd you sell your gun? In Cimarron?"

"Yes. Now, does that satisfy your curiosity?"

Grinning a lopsided grin, he said, "It's gonna take a lot to satisfy my curiosity. You're one strange woman."

"Get on that horse and go."

"There's bears in this country. Big, mean grizzlies. And if you build a fire, somebody will see the smoke and come over here to see what's going on. You need a gun."

"Hah," she snorted. "Nobody's seen this hill in over six years. You stumbled on it by accident."

"I'm betting you won't find anything. You'll need a man to ride down to Taos with you."

"I don't need a man."

"Six years? Was it six years ago?"

"Yes."

"What did they rob? Another train?"

"None of your business."

"Bet they robbed a train at Raton. A train that was carrying gold down to a bank in Santa Fe."

"You think you're smart, don't you?"

"Was it gold bricks or coins? Bricks would be easier to hide."

"I'm not saying."

"Coins. No reason for a train to be carrying bullion." He scratched his chin thoughtfully, then added, "Yup, it was coins from the mint in Denver. I've heard about that mint. Or maybe it was from another bank. Yeah, it was prob'ly from a bigger bank."

"You've got it all figured out, haven't you?"

"Not all. But I know what you're looking for."

"You could be mistaken, you know."

"I'll help you look."

"And I suppose you'll expect an equal share."

Another grin turned up one corner of his mouth. "I'll settle for a third."

"You . . ." She shut up, flustered, then said, "You . . . uh . . ." And finally, "Can I trust you?"

The grin spread over his face. "I've got the only gun and I'm bigger than you. We've been riding together for three days. Longer than that. You're a durned good-looking woman and I'm a man that likes women, and I ain't

91

bothered you. Now, ask me again if you can trust me."

"You . . . you'll settle for a third?"

"I said I would."

"Well . . . there's enough, really, for both of us. If you'll settle for a third, you can stay."

"All right," Ace Bailey said, still grinning. "Let's hobble these ponies and start looking."

Thirteen

He led the horses off the hill, unsaddled and hobbled them, then climbed back to the top. Marybelle Stewart was poking through the tall grass with the toe of her left shoe. In her baggy overalls and black hat, she looked like a boy again.

"Now tell me exactly what we're looking for," he said.

Glancing at him, she said, "You guessed right. It was gold. Gold eagles. Worth twenty dollars each."

"How much?"

"The newspaper said thirty-two thousand dollars."

"Whoa. Boy, oh boy. They hit the jackpot, didn't they?"

"Search, will you."

"Yeah, boss." He began walking slowly, head down, studying the ground. At times he squatted on his heels and parted the grass with his hands. Tiring of that, he crawled on his hands and knees, picking up rocks, putting them back. When he glanced at her, she was doing the same. Then he stood and walked over to the remains of one of the horses.

"What are you doing?"

"I don't know how heavy that many double eagles is, but I'm betting they carried it on a packhorse." He squatted again and carefully moved a leg bone, then a rib cage. A patch of dried horsehide, hair still on it, was under the ribs. Stomach queasy, he pushed the rotting skin aside with his fingers and studied the ground beneath it.

Standing again, he wiped his fingers on the seat of his pants, pushed back his black hat, and tried to think. Then he began slowly walking in circles, studying the ground. The woman stopped and watched him silently.

In widening circles, he walked around the top of the hill. For an hour he walked, never glancing up, concentrating. His stomach reminded him that he hadn't eaten since early morning and he tried to ignore it. Now he was on the side of the hill, near the top, walking, studying the ground.

She asked, "Have you got an idea?"

Without looking up, he answered, "Yeah. No. I don't know." He continued stepping a foot at a time, carefully. Suddenly, he dropped onto his hands and knees and started digging in the dirt with his fingers.

"Find something?" She hurried to him, breathing shallowly.

"Yup. It's the packsaddle. Mostly buried."

Kneeling beside him, digging with her fingers, she allowed, "It's a crossbuck saddle, all right. Now we have to find the panniers."

"They unsaddled their horses before the shooting started, and they unloaded the packhorse right here."

"Oh, I wish we had a shovel."

"We ain't even got a stick to dig with."

"Wonder why it's buried?"

"Don't know. No reason they'd bury it. Must have been the weather. Dirt and stuff washed off the top of the hill and almost covered it up."

"Yes, I suppose in six years that could have happened."

"Damn. Durn. The gold was in some panniers or pack boxes or something, and it ought to be here."

"O-o-h, my fingers are sore from digging."

"We have to have a tool of some kind."

"Why did they unsaddle their horses?"

"They must have camped here. They prob'ly knew there was some Indians on their trail, and they camped here."

He stopped digging a moment, thinking, then added, "Yeah, they had time to pile up some rocks for a fort. They knew they were in for a fight. The Indians prob'ly started shooting at daylight."

She sat up on her knees. "I can't dig with my hands any more."

He could see that her finger tips were raw and bleeding. "I'll get on a horse and ride over to those pines. I ought to find some sticks strong enough to dig with."

"We have to have something."

As he rode toward the stand of pine and fur, he was almost certain they were wasting their time. But he felt the same way he knew she felt: Now that they were here, they ought to search—and hope.

At dusk they'd broken all four of the sticks he'd found, and they finally gave up. They'd dug down a foot all around where the packsaddle had been. Digging wasn't easy in the rocky ground. At least twenty times they scratched the earth down to a rock and dug the rock out with their fingers.

Sitting back on the ground, straightening her legs in front of her, Marybelle sighed and said, "My knees are so cramped I don't think I can ever stand again. And my hands. Just look at them."

He looked. Her fingernails were broken and blood covered her fingertips. "They'll heal."

"Yes." Another long sigh came from her. "They'll heal."

Ace was sitting the same way she was, and he felt just as bad. "It just ain't here."

"No." With resignation, she added, "They took it, the Indians did. Or white men. Or whomever."

"I didn't really expect to find it."

"I thought there was a good chance."

"It was worth trying for."

"Well." She stood, stretched her legs one at a time, tested them. "It's getting dark. I'll look some more tomorrow."

Standing too, he allowed, "There's a little creek over

95

there in the pines. We'd better get over there and get a fire started before it gets plumb dark."

An hour later, their hunger sated, they sat on the ground and stared into their camp fire. He asked, "Where will you go from here?"

"Santa Fe. I've got a job there. That's where I went soon after I first saw you."

"You'll prob'ly tell me it's none of my business, but what kind of job?"

Popping pine limbs threw sparks out of their small fire while she pondered the question. A wry smile turned up the corners of her mouth. "You're so good at figuring things out, make a guess."

"Well, I'd guess you worked as a clerk of some kind, in a store or a bank or something."

She added a shrug to the wry smile. "You're half right." A pause, then, "I worked in a bank in Denver after I finished school. I worked there two years. I was fired."

He started to ask why, but instead remained silent and waited for her to go on.

"I'm not so virtuous. But that fat, bald pig of a vice president . . . whatever made him think I would go to bed with him. He . . . he fired me."

"Some bosses ain't fit to live."

Chuckling without humor, she said, "It was a good thing for him I'm not the killer you are."

He winced a little at the name "killer," but had to admit to himself he deserved it. "Yeah, that's what I am, all right."

"Anyway . . ." Now that she had started talking about herself, she went on, staring into the fire. "I've always liked the music and gaiety of the gambling and drinking establishments. I've always liked having lots of people around, dancing, laughing, and yes, even cursing. I like the night life, and I like to sleep late in the mornings. I met a man who owned a place. He hired me to be a hostess." A pause, a glance at him, and, "My job was to circulate,

96

glad-hand everybody, be cheerful, and" — another glance at him — "sleep with the boss."

Ace stood, broke a dead tree limb by stomping on it, and put it in the fire. He watched the flames wrap themselves around it, then sat down again.

"I'm not a whore. I've never been to bed with a man I didn't like. But . . . as I said, I'm not just breaking out with virtue."

In a low, emotionless tone, he said, "It's none of my business." Then he tried to make a joke of it. "Like a feller said, 'It's a good thing I wasn't born a female; there'd sure be a whore in the family.' "

The joke fell flat.

"I've never cheated anyone. And although I accompanied my dad when he robbed trains, I didn't do the robbing myself. But I wasn't cut out for a dull clerical job. And the last thing I want is a husband and some kids to raise."

He realized that the best thing he could do then was to keep quiet.

"After I first met you I went to Cimarron flat broke. By selling my rifle, I had enough to buy a few groceries and spend a couple of days looking for that hill. Of course I didn't find it. From here I rode on to Santa Fe, sold my horse and cleaned myself up, then got a job in a place called The Red Rose. It was the same kind of job I had in Denver. Same deal. I read about your arrest in a newspaper. I just had to try to find the gold."

The fire popped, crackled, threw sparks. Her face had a kind of eerie look in the dancing firelight.

He said, "It was six years ago, that robbery. What took you so long?"

I didn't know about the robbery until a few weeks ago. My dad had a habit of disappearing for years at a time. The last time I saw him he was a little . . . uh . . . put out with me. Said he didn't send me to school so I could work in a saloon. But after he was gone six years, I became

97

worried and started looking for him. If he was dead, I wanted to know about it."

Staring into the fire, he wondered how he'd feel about her father if he were in her place.

"I didn't love him the way most women love their dads," Marybelle continued. "He shouldn't have taken me along when he was riding the outlaw trails. But he did try to make up for it by sending me to school. He always paid my tuition and board, either in person or by mail. I never had to worry about that. I owe him."

After a long silence, she said, "I'm going to have to get a shovel and bury those skeletons. I can't leave my dad's remains exposed like that."

"I'll help you."

She flashed a smile across the flames. "I'm talking on and on, aren't I? It must be the isolation. And the quiet night. Now you know all you want to know about Marybelle Stewart. More than you want to know."

Shaking his head, he said, "Uh-uh. I've never met anyone like you. I've met some women, but none like you. Uh . . . before you run out of words, tell me how you found out about the robbery."

"Easy. The newspapers. I traveled to just about every city where I thought my dad might be or had been. In Santa Fe, I asked if he was in prison there. I had to name him. A deputy recognized the name and told me about a Tobe Stewart who was a suspect in an old train robbery in Raton. He looked up a wanted reader and gave me the exact date. Then all I had to do was go to the newspaper and look through the papers that were printed back then."

"Well, I'll be durned. I wouldn't have thought of that."

"Four men hid their horses behind a warehouse, broke open a safe in the mail car, tied up the one man on guard, and were gone before anyone was the wiser. The guard recognized Tobe Stewart, my dad."

"Well, I'll be durned."

"Anyway, I'll ride to that store in Angel in the morning

98

and use one of my last few dollars to buy a shovel." Chuckling without humor, she added, "Who knows? While I'm digging a grave, I might uncover a cache of gold."

"We have to give it our best try."

"We?"

"Yeah. While you're gone, I'll keep on looking."

Fourteen

Though he knew it was useless, he crawled all over the knoll on his hands and knees, examining every rock and blade of grass. It was nearly noon when she came back, carrying a long-handled shovel across the saddle in front of her.

He said, "I'll bet you got some curious stares."

"Yes, but I'm getting used to that. When a man asked what I needed a shovel for, I pretended I didn't hear him. He didn't ask again."

"It's not every day a woman dressed the way you are goes in a store and buys a shovel. In fact," Bailey grinned a lopsided grin, "it's not every day you see a woman dressed the way you are."

He took the shovel, looked for the softest part of the hill, and began digging. It wasn't easy in the rocky ground. He dug up as much rocks as dirt, and it took an hour and a half to dig a hole four feet long, three feet wide, and two feet deep. Resting, leaning on the shovel handle, he said, "We don't have to worry about the coyotes digging them up."

"No. This is probably deep enough."

They gathered bones, skulls, and pieces of rotten clothing. When they had the skulls arranged at one end and the rib cages and leg bones at the other end, Bailey shoveled dirt back into the hole.

"I never could understand it," he said. "I've dug fence post holes and everything, and even when I put back every speck of dirt I took out, there was never enough dirt to refill the hole."

"It wouldn't do to leave a depression."

"Nope. I'll have to dig up some sod to level the ground here. Maybe leave a little mound."

"I wish we had something to make a marker out of."

"There's plenty of rocks."

Marybelle Stewart, walking in her baggy overalls, gathered rocks while Ace dug sod from another section of the hill to fill the grave. Then they piled the rocks a foot high at the head end.

"What will we do with the shovel?" she asked. "I'm not about to carry it back."

"Me either. Let's stick it in the ground at the head of the grave. Someday somebody'll see it and the marker and wonder who is buried here."

"They'll never guess." Pensive a moment, she glanced at Bailey. "Seems like we ought to say something over the grave. They were human beings, and one was my father. You said your father is a church pastor. Do you know anything to say?"

"Well, I've never done this before, but I guess I could say something."

They stood over the grave with their hats off. Her chestnut hair fell to her shoulders; his straw-colored hair was uncombed and thick over his ears. In a mumble, he recited the Lord's Prayer, something he had been taught by the Reverend Bailey a long time ago.

Then it was time to part.

"You sure you don't want me to ride to Taos with you?"

"No. I've been over that road by myself before. You can keep the horse and half of the groceries. That will leave me enough to get back to civilization. I have only a few dollars left, but you can have half."

"No, I don't want any money. You've done enough for me."

"Where will you go?"

"Back home. But I'll have to take a long way around and come down from the north. They're prob'ly looking for me east and west."

101

"You'll starve before you can travel that far."

"Naw. I can shoot a buckskin or a rabbit or something. Maybe I'll come across a ranch or a sheepherder's camp and work for some grub."

They mounted and rode back to their camp in the trees. There, she began separating the groceries and camp supplies. "You can take the coffeepot. I'm not that crazy about coffee."

"Naw, you take it. It's yours."

"You have to have something to cook out of."

"Just give me some matches, and if you've got any salt left, I'd like to have some of that."

"You sure you won't take some money?"

"Naw."

"Shall we eat something before we go?"

"Naw. I'll save my share."

His share was a pound slab of bacon, a pound of jerky, and four tins of fruit. He had a blanket and a piece of a tarp to roll it in and tie behind the cantle of his well-worn saddle.

Ready to leave now, she held out her hand to shake. "I wish you luck, Ace Bailey. If you happen over Santa Fe way and need a place to . . . to keep out of sight for a few days, look me up. I'll probably be at The Red Rose."

He shook her hand. "Thanks for helping me bust out of jail. You saved my life, and I'd sure like to return the favor, but" — he looked down — "I don't offhand know of a way to do it."

"You have already. I'm not leaving here rich as I'd hoped, but I did find out what happened to my father and gave him a decent burial. I feel better about that. And, who knows, maybe our paths will cross again one day."

Still looking down, he said, "Yeah, maybe."

She mounted her horse. *"Adios,* Ace."

"Adios, Marybelle."

She rode away, angling south and east to pick up the wagon road to Taos. He watched her a long moment, then stepped into the saddle. "Well, pardner," he said to the horse, "there's plenty of grass and you won't go hungry, but you've

102

got a few hills to climb." Turning the horse north, he rode out of the timber, crossed a broad vega, and started up a pine-studded mountain ridge. There was no trail and he had to traverse the hill, almost doubling back on himself at times. Huge granite boulders seemed to grow out of the side of the hill. The sweet smell of pine and fur filled his nostrils. His plan was to get into the San Luis Valley of Colorado and turn east. He could only hope he'd eventually come across a trail of some kind and find the easiest way over the Sangre de Cristos. Once he got over the mountains, traveling would be easy. But he didn't know how many high, steep hills he'd have to climb to get there.

It was close to sundown when he got to the top of the first rocky ridge. Pausing to let the horse get its wind, he looked to the north and downhill to a narrow grassy valley. Beyond that was another high, rocky pine-covered hill. "Down there," he said, "is a good place to camp, feller. There's water and grass and everything you want."

At the bottom of the ridge he crossed a dim trail that went east and west, east toward the wagon road and the settlements of Eagle Nest and Angel. It was an old trail that had once been well used but now was almost grown over with tall wheat grass. Reining up beside it, Bailey shook his head. "Damn. Wonder where it comes from. Sure wish it was going my way." He reined his horse west and followed the trail, hoping it turned north somewhere and went over the mountains. Just before dark, he saw the cabin.

"Now I know where it came from," he said to himself. "Wonder who lives there."

When he got to the cabin, he realized that no one lived there. The structure was made of logs cut out of the nearby woods, but one wall had fallen in and only half the roof remained. He rode up cautiously, keeping his right hand near the Colt. At the cabin, he stayed on his horse and studied everything carefully. The floor was of time-warped boards, broken in places. A pack rat had built a nest in one corner under what remained of the roof. A rusted sheet metal stove sat tilted in another corner, with a section of stovepipe sticking out of it. More sections of stovepipe had fallen beside it. A narrow wooden cot squatted under the sky, with pieces of the collapsed roof on top of it. A few ragged pieces of clothing hung on nails driven into the walls.

After a long look around, Ace knew he was alone. A pole corral had been built across a narrow stream, but only half the posts still stood and most of the poles were down. A lean-to built of pine poles stood crookedly at one end of the corral. Somebody had lived here, but not lately. Dismounting, he dropped the reins and stepped past a wooden door that hung crookedly on leather hinges. Whoever had lived here had moved out in a hurry. Torn sacks of coffee, flour, and sugar had been knocked off shelves, probably by pack rats, and a coffeepot, an iron skillet, and an iron cooking pot littered the floor under a collapsed wooden shelf. There was a small table and one chair, both made of sections of aspen trunks. One leg of the table had given way, and a tin plate and cup had slid off it onto the floor. The chair didn't look strong enough to sit on.

Rat excrement was mixed with the sugar and flour.

Dark was coming on fast, and Bailey led the horse to the creek that ran behind the cabin and let it drink its fill. Then he unsaddled and hobbled the animal. "If you see any ghosts, pardner, remember that the dead can't hurt you."

He helped himself to a stack of firewood inside the cabin and built a fire outside, near the door. For a moment he considered scooping up a handful of the spilled coffee and boiling it in the coffeepot. "Naw," he said aloud. "Too old. Can't be any good." He let the fire die down to a bed of hot ashes, then put in two thick strips of bacon. When the bacon sizzled and curled, he fished it out with a stick, blew the ashes off, and ate with his fingers. The jerky wasn't any easier to chew and swallow than it was before, but he got some of it down, then finished his meal with a can of peaches.

Lying wrapped in his one blanket and piece of tarp, looking at the sky, Bailey speculated on who had lived here. Whoever he was, he had lived alone. There was only one chair, one plate, and one cup. And he had left without taking everything of value with him.

Or had he left?

Maybe he had died. Broken his leg or got sick or something and died.

Or maybe he had been killed by Indians, the same bunch of renegades that had killed Marybelle's father. If so, his remains should be around here somewhere.

Sure. The Indians had ransacked the cabin and taken the man's guns, horses, and everything else of value to them. That would explain it.

But why wasn't he missed? The trail went east from here, and he had to have traded at either Eagle Nest or Angel. Somebody knew him and where he lived. If not exactly, then about where he lived. Somebody should have come looking for him.

Well, hell, maybe somebody did and had packed his remains away to be buried. But why hadn't the stove and other stuff been taken? The stove would be hard to tie onto a packhorse, but it could be done. Whoever had lived here had done it. There were no wagon tracks. Well, maybe whoever found him didn't have a packhorse.

Maybe . . . Aw, hell.

Either the man's remains were buried in a cemetery or his bones were somewhere near the cabin.

"Lord," Ace Bailey mumbled to himself, "I've seen all the human bones I want to see for a long time."

But in the morning, he'd have to have another look.

Fifteen

The bay horse was grazing near the creek when Ace Bailey unwrapped himself at dawn. Before he pulled on his boots he held them upside down and shook them. No telling what might have crawled into them during the night. The boots were cold and uncomfortable, and he had to walk a ways to get the feel of them again. Nothing had changed. No ghost had disturbed anything. Looking inside the cabin, he saw a grey pack rat run down one of the walls, its unblinking brown eyes fixed on him.

"I won't bother you if you don't bother me," he said aloud.

Next, he checked the horse to be sure the hobbles weren't making its ankles and pasterns sore, then went to the creek and splashed water over his face. The water was cold, and he shivered.

His breakfast was more bacon cooked on the end of a stick over an open fire. The stick burned off before the bacon was done, and he again had to blow ashes off his food before he could eat it.

He murmured, "A little clean ashes never hurt anybody."

But the bacon was beginning to smell rancid. It wouldn't keep another twenty-four hours.

Breakfast over, he began his search for human remains, walking in widening circles around the cabin. It didn't take long.

The grave was across the creek near a big ponderosa, in

a grassy spot where the digging was easy. The length and width of the mound, together with the small pile of rocks at one end, told him it was a human grave, almost hidden in the grass and wild rosebushes. There was no headstone, nothing to identify the deceased.

"Rest in peace," Bailey said, then went to saddle his horse.

He followed the trail west for a mile, where it petered out. Now it was climb another mountain, and then another and another. He wished he knew this country and was familiar with an easier route.

By mid afternoon he decided he'd have to change directions. Ahead of him, to the north, was a ridge so high and steep it would take all day to climb it. The horse was tiring.

"You've been good to me, feller," Bailey said. "Wish I could make it easier on you."

He stopped in another narrow grassy valley beside another small stream, which was fed by snow runoff from the divide to the north. The country here was too high for cottonwoods and oaks. The only leaves were on the aspens, the willow bushes that grew along the stream, and an acre of bushy cinquefoil, sporting tiny yellow flowers. There was a trail of sorts—dim, narrow, and hard to see in most places. It was a game trail, and it could go anywhere.

The horse was glad to get the saddle off, and Bailey could see that it wanted to lie down and roll and scratch its back. He plucked a double handful of grass and scratched the animal's back himself.

He broke off enough willow branches to build a fire, then cut off the grey spots from his small slab of bacon.

When he finished doing that, he looked up and realized he was being watched.

It was a bear. A big silvertip. So named because its long, brownish-yellow hair was tipped by a silvery white. It had come out of the timber and was angling toward the creek when it smelled and saw Ace Bailey and the horse.

As big as it was it could kill the horse, and the man and his .38 caliber pistol wouldn't be much more than a small inconvenience.

Bailey had seen only one silvertip before, and he'd been warned not to shoot. The brutes were protected by thick hides and rolls of fat that could absorb anything but high-powered rifle bullets. And even if shot with a high-powered bullet, the bear would probably live long enough to tear the hell out of things.

All Bailey could do was sit still and hope the brute wasn't mad at anybody.

It was standing on all fours, looking awkward with its forefeet shorter than its hind ones. Bailey had been warned that in spite of its awkward appearance, a silvertip could run surprisingly fast for a short distance.

The horse had sensed the bear and was hopping nervously with its forefeet hobbled, trying to get farther away from it. Bailey had to protect his horse. But how to do it?

Moving slowly, he drew the .38 and waited. If he had to shoot, he decided, he'd shoot for the brain. Pump as many bullets into the bear's head as he could. He waited, breathing in shallow breaths.

The bear stood still, its small round ears erect, its small eyes taking in the man and the horse.

It had a nose like a hound dog and it sniffed the air, trying to decide whether the strange animals before it were something to swat aside. It took two steps closer to the horse to get a better smell.

Slowly, watching the bear, Bailey went to the horse. He spoke softly. "Easy, pardner. Don't try to run away. I don't know if I can keep him off you, but I'll damned sure try. Easy, now."

Then the bear stood on its hind legs, still sniffing.

Bailey muttered, "Oh boy. Damn, damn, damn." He wished he'd had his bridle with him so he could take the hobbles off and lead the horse away, but his saddle and bridle were near the camp fire. If he took the hobbles off now, the horse would run away and he'd be afoot. "Whoa, feller. Whoa, now."

Moving its huge head from side to side, the bear let a rumble out of its throat. It stood a good seven feet high. Bailey waited. Watched and waited.

Then the brute arched its neck and rumbled again. The long fur on the back of its neck was stiff and straight.

And suddenly it dropped to all fours and ran—right at Bailey and the horse. Ran fast.

Bailey raised his pistol, getting the bear's mouth in the sights. Don't shoot unless you have to, he'd been warned. Bullets only make a bear angrier. Angrier? Hell, the brute was already in a killing mood.

He waited, intending to make the shots count.

The bear was thirty feet away. Twenty feet. The horse was going crazy, trying to run with its forefeet hobbled.

POP, went the .38. POP, POP, POP.

The bear continued on, as if it hadn't felt the bullets.

POP, POP. The Colt snapped on a spent shell.

Ten feet.

Run, Ace Bailey, his mind screamed. Run, you fool. He stood there, waiting for a blow from a powerful paw.

And as suddenly as it had started running, the bear stopped. It sat on its haunches and dragged a huge paw across its eyes. With a long groan, it fell onto its side. The legs stiffened, and the huge body quivered.

Then it was still.

For a long moment Bailey was quiet, feeling numb. He said, "Whoa. Gaw-ud damn." Not taking any chances, he quickly punched out the empty shells and reloaded the .38 with cartridges from his belt. When he turned to the horse, it was on its side. Terror had caused it to throw itself down in an effort to get away.

"Gaw-ud damn," Bailey said again. "Can you get up, feller?" The horse got its hobbled forefeet out in front and heaved itself up. Trembling, it stood there while Bailey walked around it, looking for injuries. He rubbed the horse's neck and talked in a low tone until it quit trembling, then he went to the bear.

It was a beautiful animal—had been—with its thick, silver-tipped fur and shaggy head. Speaking aloud, Ace said, "Too bad you had such a short temper, mister bear. If you'd just left us alone, you'd still be big and purty instead of dead and bleeding."

Just the smell of the bear made the horse nervous, and Bailey decided to move camp. With the fire out and everything packed, he swung into the saddle and tried to decide which way to go. He had to get around that high, steep mountain ahead of him, but which way was the best?

He turned the horse west.

As he rode he talked to himself. "It'd make a damned fine pelt. But naw, it'd take all day to skin it, and when I got it skinned, this horse couldn't carry it and me, too. Some folks would give a lot for that pelt. Too bad."

The game trail petered out, reappeared, then petered out again. It went where the deer and elk wanted to go, not where Ace Bailey wanted to go. He camped again in the same narrow valley two miles from the dead bear. The bacon was on the edge of being spoiled, so he ate it all rather than throw some of it away later.

In the morning he rode on west, looking up at the mountain. Not until the sun was near its peak did he see an end to it. The mountain sloped down a mile or so ahead, and Bailey's spirits picked up. "That's got to be an easier way," he said to the horse. And when he got there, he discovered he was right.

The mountain sloped down to a curve in the valley and into twenty acres of willow bushes. Pushing through the willows would be easier than climbing mountains. But Bailey stopped there and let the horse rest while he ate a can of apricots. When he was mounted again, he spoke to the animal.

"Well, old feller, for a change it's gonna be harder on me than you. Let's go see what's on the other side of these bushes. Hell, who knows, we might find a good road with no hills to climb."

It wasn't easy. The horse, being lower, had no trouble pushing its way through, but the man took a beating. Willow branches pulled at his arms and shoulders and slapped at his face. When his hat was dragged off he had to stop, dismount, put it back on, and remount. He couldn't see ten feet ahead, and he hoped he wasn't going in a circle. Now he knew why some Texas cowboys wore those leather wrist cuffs. With his right hand in front of his face, his shirtsleeve was pulled back and his wrist was scratched and bleeding.

This was worse than those damned Texas mesquites. He was glad he didn't have to drive a herd of cattle through here.

Finally, he broke out of the willows, and when he did he heard cattle bawling.

There was no mistaking the sound. He'd heard it many times. Somewhere ahead cattle were bawling and men were yelling and whistling.

Some cow outfit was moving a herd through this valley, and they weren't far ahead.

Bailey paused. It was nearing sundown. Whoever was moving the cattle had to get them in a bunch before dark. Would they recognize him? Naw. Not likely. Should he ride to meet them? Why not. They would have to invite him to supper, and boy could he use a good meal. Not only that, but perhaps they could show him the best way over the mountains to Colorado.

Wiping his eyes with a shirtsleeve and resetting his hat, Bailey said aloud, "Well, hell, pardner, let's go see what there is to see."

Sixteen

He picked up a trail on the far side of the willows, and traveling was easy. A mile from the willows the valley widened into a broad vega with steep slopes on each side, and that's where the cattle were. Cowboys had the herd gathered now and were holding them in a bunch to keep them from wandering away. The slopes were covered by thick growths of spruce, pine, and aspens. It would take some night riding to keep the cattle out in the open country.

Ace Bailey reined up and sat his saddle while he counted five men. He estimated there were about six hundred cattle, all longhorns of every color and all dry stuff, prime beeves. The five men had their work cut out for them, getting that many cattle through the mountains.

Touching spurless boot heels to the horse, he rode forward at a slow walk. Some of the cowboys watched him approach, and when he was closer, one man rode toward him.

"Howdy."

"Howdy."

"You traveling?" The man was all cowboy, lean as a whip, with a flat-brimmed grey hat pulled down to his eyebrows. He wore a leather vest and leather stovepipe chaps. His face was as leathery as his vest. He sat solidly in his saddle, and he appeared to be a man who could handle any kind of horse.

"Yeah," Ace said. "I'm going up to Colorado, the San Luis Valley, but I'm a stranger in these hills and I'm not sure I'm taking the best route."

"That you ain't." His squinty eyes took in the .38 in its low-slung holster.

"Maybe you can show me the way."

"You lookin' for work?"

"Well," Ace said, thoughtfully, "I'm not looking. But I can see you're shorthanded.

"Had any experience with a cattle herd?"

Grinning, Ace said, "I've been up the trail from West Texas to Kansas a couple of times."

"You're right, I'm shorthanded. Had to fire two men back yonder. If I'd knowed they was boozers and had whiskey with 'em, I'd of never hired 'em." After a pause, he went on, "I'd guess from your saddle that you ain't exactly flush with money. I'll pay you a dollar six-bits a day and keep you mounted on good horses. My cook feeds good."

"Where are you going?"

"Over to the flatlands south of Raton. I'm ramrodding the Cross Seven outfit and my boss has some land over there. These beefs will get fat there and we'll ship 'em out of Raton in the fall."

"The Cross Seven? Where's that?"

"We come from Cerro Questa, this side of the Rio Grande. We're goin' on east to Bobcat Pass, then down onto the plains under the Raton Mountains."

"You going anywhere near Cimarron or Raton?"

"Naw. We'll stay north of Cimarron and south of Raton."

Bailey studied the herd, the cowboys, the remuda and chuck wagon farther back in the valley. The herd wasn't going where he wanted to go, but he needed the pay and the chuck. "I can use the work," he said finally.

113

"My name's Potter, Adam Potter." He waited for Bailey to introduce himself.

"Alvin Bailey."

"Understand somethin', Bailey. If you're wanted by the law, don't tell none of us. And if the law comes lookin' for you, we ain't gonna lie to 'em. And if you ever draw that there six-shooter, you'll have the whole outfit on you. Is that understood?"

Nodding, Bailey said, "Yeah."

"Then let's go back to the remuda and catch you a fresh horse. Your work begins right now." With a slow grin, Adam Potter added, "If I was you, I wouldn't do any ropin' out of that saddle."

"No," Bailey grinned with him. "I'll have to let somebody else do the roping. I never was too handy with a catch rope, anyhow."

At the remuda, Adam Potter nodded at the wrangler and said, "We need old Hoppy right now. Hold 'em up over yonder 'til the boys catch their night horses." The wrangler, a cowboy with a wrinkled, weathered face and grey hair showing under his hat, merely nodded.

The boss took his rope down and shook out a loop. He rode into the herd of horses slowly, carefully, not wanting to spook them. When he was close enough to the animal he wanted, he pitched his loop with one smooth, swift overhanded throw. The loop shot out, turned over in the air, and dropped over the head of a chunky brown gelding. He held the animal tied to his saddle horn until Bailey got the saddle and bridle off his horse and got the bridle onto the brown one.

"You can turn your horse in with the remuda," Potter said. "Go pick a spot with the herd. We're gonna have to do some nighthawkin', and after chuck I'll decide who spells who."

Bailey saddled the brown gelding, mounted, and rode at a trot to the herd. He approached a cowboy wearing

114

batwing chaps and a ragged black hat, and said, "Howdy."

"Howdy. You just hire on?" The cowboy eyed the Colt .38 and the worn-out saddle.

"Yep."

"The boss said to let 'em scatter a little and graze, but keep 'em out of the timber." The cowboy turned his horse away and took up another position.

Ace Bailey had his position with the herd now, and he knew the other men expected him to keep it. Cowboys working a herd never rode around each other. The brown horse was a little tough in the mouth but moved fast enough when Bailey had to turn back a spotted longhorn steer. He got on the other side of the steer as fast as he could, turned it back, then reined up and let the animal trot back to the herd.

Other men watched him and realized he knew what he was doing.

He was on first guard that night, and he ate supper with two other cowboys. Sitting cross-legged on the ground, holding a tin plate on his knees, he stuffed himself with beef, beans, biscuits, and a wedge of pie made with dried apples.

One of the cowboys said, "I see you're travelin' light. What'd you say your name is?"

"Alvin Bailey."

"Bailey? I've heard that name some'eres. Any kin of Ace Bailey?"

"My name is Alvin Charles Bailey."

The others knew from the tone of his voice he wasn't going to say any more on that subject.

"I've got one more blanket than I need, Alvin. I'll loan it to you. This ground gets purty hard and cold."

"I can spare a blanket, too," the other man said. "You'll need 'em."

"I appreciate it." Standing, Bailey scraped his plate and

put it in a tub of water beside the chuck wagon. He put his bridle and saddle on a bald-faced black horse the boss pointed out to him, then rode back to the herd.

With the two borrowed blankets, he slept better that night than he had in a long time, and at first light he was up, splashing water on his face. While he ate hotcakes and cured ham and drank scalding black coffee, he said conversationally, "I guess you fellers know about that bunch of willows ahead."

"Yeah, we know. It ain't gonna be no Sunday school picnic."

"Hell," said a grey-haired cowboy, "them willers're nothin'. You fellers should of been with me when I was chousin' bulls out of them canyons in northern Arizoney. You couldn't cut through that brush with a axe. I mean it took chaps, taps, and latigo straps just to look at 'em."

"Sure, Willy," a cowboy grinned. "I expect you'll show us all how to do it."

A picnic it wasn't. It took nearly all day to get six hundred cattle through about twenty acres of dense bushes. The cattle put their heads down and plowed through the brush with ease, going wherever they wanted, while to the men on horseback, moving was slow and torturous. To make matters worse, some of the cattle got on the other side of a creek where the ground was boggy but, with their split hooves, had little trouble getting over the bogs. The horses, however, sunk in to their knees, and had to hump and buck to get out.

The whole crew changed mounts at noon, then worked at it again, yelling, whistling, and cursing. Finally, an hour before sundown, they were on the other side. Adam Potter ordered the horse wrangler to bring up the remuda so the crew could change horses again, and he ordered the crew to keep the herd moving until they were a mile from the willows. There, just before dark, they got the herd milling. Two of the cowboys went back to help the cook get his wagon through. Supper was late, but Adam Potter wasn't letting the crew go to supper anyway until the herd was quiet, spread out, and grazing.

Ace Bailey and two others ate hurriedly and quietly so they could get back to the herd and relieve the others. Riding back, Bailey told Willy about the bear he'd killed. "You say his carcass is in this valley?" Willy asked. "That's somethin' I gotta see."

The rest of the crew couldn't believe it when Willy reported what he'd seen. "A sure 'nuff silvertip?" a cowboy asked. "I've seen only two of 'em in my life. They're big enough to kill a buffalo, and they can get mean."

"This 'un was purt' near as big as a hoss," Willy said.

"What'd you shoot 'im with, Alvin? That pistol you're packin'?"

"This is all I've got. I emptied the gun at him, and he was close enough that I couldn't miss."

"Hit 'im at least five times. Two shots knocked out some teeth, another'n knocked out his left eye, and at least two more hit 'im square between the eyes."

"Some shootin'."

"There's a purty hide," Willy said. "Say, Alvin, wanta help me skin 'im? We can sell that hide."

"Naw. I'll leave that to whoever wants it."

Willy and another cowboy got permission from Adam Potter to take the time to skin the dead bear. "But don't be too long at it," Potter said. "You have to catch up with us before we start over the divide. We're gonna need all the help we can get."

The cook, a wiry man with a walrus moustache and a bill cap, grudgingly allowed the two to take some salt to preserve the pelt. "But," he said, "if you gents don't get enough salt in your chuck, don't blame me."

"Are we going over that mountain?" Bailey asked.

"Yeah," Potter answered. "We're going down this valley

117

to where the ridge ain't quite so high and steep, but we're goin' over it. And then we're goin' over Bobcat Pass. And after that we're gonna cross the Vermejo River north of Cimarron."

"You're gonna earn your pay, Alvin," a cowboy grinned. "I'm glad you came along."

They got six hundred cattle over the first ridge, horses clambering over rocks, and when they got to the top, four men went back to help get the chuck wagon up. Two tied the ends of their catch ropes to one side of the wagon and wrapped the other ends around their saddle horns to keep the wagon from turning over. The other two tied their ropes to the front of the wagon. With four harness horses and two saddle horses pulling, they got the wagon over the ridge.

For a day after that traveling was easy along the bottom of another mountain valley, then came Bobcat Pass, and the clambering, sliding, cursing, and yelling began again.

Finally they were out of the mountains and crossing the shallow Vermejo River.

That night when the crew was feeling good about the job they'd done and were gathered near the cook's fire, Bailey told them about the remains of a cabin and a grave he'd seen. Immediately, Adam Potter stood and walked away.

"He don't want to talk about it," a cowboy said. "He helped hang 'im."

"It was old Tate," another put in. "A hoss thief, Injun lover, and all-round no-good sumbitch."

"That describes 'im, sure 'nuff. No matter how many white men, women, and kids them runagades killed and scalped, old Tate traded with 'em. He'd buy guns and sell 'em to the Injuns for double his money."

"If the Injuns had any money."

"He finally stole too many hosses from the Cross

118

Seven, and Adam and some others caught 'im with 'em. That was all the evidence they needed."

"I wasn't one of 'em, but I heared about it. They didn't put a marker on his grave 'cause Tate is the only name they knowed 'im by and they wasn't sure that was his real name."

Bailey said, "How long ago was this?"

"Oh, let's see, 'bout six years, I'd reckon. There was some of them runagades on a killin' spree back then, and Adam figures Tate was tradin' with 'em."

"It was Victorio and a bunch of Mescaleros. They kilt a lot of folks before they was run down to Mexico."

"Some folks think Victorio never got this far north."

"It was him. I'd bet on it."

Bailey rolled up in his blankets and went to sleep that night, thinking about a renegade Indian named Victorio, four dead train robbers, an abandoned cabin, and a grave near it.

Next morning the sky was clear in the east but cloudy in the west, and the cowboys figured it would rain about the middle of the afternoon. Bailey finished his breakfast, scraped his plate, and started to the remuda to catch a horse. Adam Potter intercepted him.

"Alvin," the cowboy boss said somberly, "we've got easy travelin' from here on, and you can leave if you want to. I'll give you an extra day's pay."

Bailey sensed that the boss, and the rest of the crew for that matter, knew who he was, and Potter wanted him gone in case lawmen came asking questions.

"I'll make that two extra days' pay," Potter said. "You came along when we needed you and you've been a good hand. I don't feel right about sendin' you on your way now that the hard work is done."

"I appreciate it," Bailey said. "I changed my mind about going to Colorado. Guess I'll head south to Albu-kirk."

He tried to give back the two blankets he'd borrowed, but the cowboys refused. "You'll need 'em, Alvin."

So, after saying *adios,* Bailey mounted his horse and rode south. But only so far as to be out of sight. Then he unsaddled and hobbled the horse.

"Albukirk, hell," he said to himself. "That's the last place I want to go right now. I've got to get home. Got a job to do."

Seventeen

The cowboys had been right. It rained that afternoon. Thunder boomed and lightning cracked. Rain came down in sheets. Ace Bailey wrapped the piece of tarp around his shoulders, sat on a rock, and kept from getting soaked. The rain didn't last long. After dark he ate some of the cold steaks and biscuits the cook had given him, then saddled his horse.

By the light of a half-moon he rode northeast, staying wide around where he figured the Cross Seven outfit would be. Ace and the horse were both stronger now, and he enjoyed riding on the flatlands in the pale light. Mount Capulin was his destination.

He rode all night, and by dawn he saw his uncle's cabin and corrals ahead. Reining up, he studied the layout. Only one horse was in the corral, and darned if it wasn't the black horse he'd traded for way back in Arroyo Hondo. Another saddle horse and a harness team grazed nearby. A field of Indian corn was ripening behind the cabin. Uncle Amos was at home and alone.

While he watched, the cabin door opened and Uncle Amos came out, fastening the elastic suspenders that held his pants up over a round belly. Straight grey hair hung down his face as he dragged a shirtsleeve across his eyes.

Ace yelled, "Hyo-o-o," stood in his stirrups, and waved his hat.

Uncle Amos's head swiveled in that direction. He blinked, squinted, wiped his eyes again.

"Hyo-o-o, Uncle Amos."

The grey-whiskered face split into a grin. He waved and motioned Ace forward. Ace came up on a gallop, then sat his horse, grinning.

"Danged if it ain't you, Alvin. Never expected to see you alive again. That danged sheriff must of had twenty riders lookin' for you, and ever' danged one of 'em had blood in his eyes. How in hell did you get away, anyhow? Put that horse in the pen and come on in this house."

Inside, the older man got a fire going in the two-burner cast-iron stove and put some water on to boil. He asked again, "How in hell did you get away?"

"I had some help," Ace said. "How are Mom and Pop? Heard anything from them?"

The smile left Uncle Amos's face. "Your pop's in jail, and your mom is havin' a hard time. Can't work the farm by herself. Ever'thing is goin' to hell."

Anger swept through Ace Bailey. Cold fury started in his stomach and worked its way up to his throat. He muttered through his teeth, "Why is Pop in jail?"

"They thought it was him that slipped you a gun and helped you bust out of jail. He's s'posed to get a trial, but he ain't got one yet."

"It wasn't Pop. It was somebody else. That goddamn sheriff knows damned well it wasn't Pop."

"I know it wasn't and your mom knows it wasn't."

"That son of a bitch. That goddamn son of a bitch. He's got to die."

"Now don't go runnin' off in all directions, Alvin. That sheriff's got hisself surrounded with tough deputies all the time. Hell, they say he even sleeps with 'em. What nobody can figure out is what he's payin' 'em with."

"He's a goddamn thief. He's a thief and a liar and a killer."

"Yeah, I can't argue about that, but don't you go lopin' over there with the intention of shootin' 'im full of holes. You might get him, but them deputies'll get you."

Ace's words came out in a hiss, "He's got to die."

"Yeah, but you're young. You don't wanta swap your life for his."

They were quiet. Anger seethed through Ace. He stood, stomped to the door, looked out, sat again, stood again. His jaw muscles bulged. The older man watched him without speaking, knowing there was nothing he could say that would settle the anger.

Finally, Ace said, "When was the last time the deputies were here?"

"They came by again only two days ago."

"I can't stay here, then."

"You're safe here for a day or two."

"Do you know if they went over and bothered Mindy?"

"Don't think they know about Mindy. At least, they never mentioned her."

That took some of the anger out of Ace, calming him a little. But not much. Uncle Amos dumped a handful of coffee into the pot, let it resume boiling, then poured some cold water in to settle the grounds. He poured hot coffee into two tin cups. "I'll mix some pancakes and we'll eat."

While they ate hotcakes smothered with dark sorghum, Uncle Amos said, "Ever'body in the territory knows about you. Ever'time I go over to Raton, I read about you in the newspaper."

Swallowing, then taking a sip of hot coffee, Ace said, "I wish I could let it all lie. I've had enough of this sleeping on the ground, going hungry, riding at night."

"You're gonna have to go away, Alvin. Far away."

"Maybe I will. But not yet."

"Right now is a good time. Ever'body thinks you're long gone."

"Not yet."

"Well, if you're bound and determined to go back to Stockwell County, do some studyin' on it. Figure out what you're gonna do and how you're gonna do it."

"Yeah. I can't just ride up to the sheriff's office and start shooting. First thing I have to do is see Mom."

"Keep out of sight. If I was you, I'd come down from the north, from Colorado."

"That's what I figured to do, but I'm tired of riding over mountains."

"It's the long way around, but the safest way. Go over the Trinchera Pass. There ain't hardly any traffic on that pass anymore."

"Wonder if I'd be safe here today. I could use some shut-eye, and that bay horse could use some good feed."

"I'll feed your horse. You flop down on that there bed. I s'pose you recognized that black horse in the corral. Your mother asked me to take 'im. She ain't got enough feed for her own stock."

"I'll swap you. The bay's climbed his share of mountains, and his shoes are getting thin."

"The black horse is rarin' to go and he's standin' on good iron."

"Take good care of the bay. He's worked hard for me."

"You know I will, Alvin. Your mom thinks you inherited your love of horses from me."

Grinning for the first time since he arrived, Ace said, "Some folks think I like horses better than people, and that ain't too far from the truth."

"I feel the same way sometimes."

He took a bath out of a washtub while his uncle stayed outside and kept a lookout. The rest of the day he slept. In the evening he saddled the black horse with his own saddle, tied his blankets behind the cantle, and mounted.

Uncle Amos said, "Goin' over the mountains'll make it a longer ride. You'll prob'ly get home tomorrow about dark. If I was you, I'd keep that horse in the barn out of sight. Your mother'll be glad to see you."

A three-quarter moon lighted the way over the Raton Mountains. Once used by cattle drovers who refused to pay the toll over the Raton Pass, the Trinchera Pass was

124

a good route for a horsebacker but impassable for a wagon. On the north side was Colorado, a genuine, bona fide state of the Union. At dawn, Bailey unsaddled, ate cold biscuits and bacon, then spent three hours sleeping within sight of Trinchera Creek, east of Raton Mesa. Before noon he resaddled the black horse and rode on east, traveling at a slow, steady trot, keeping on the north side of the mountains. By late afternoon the mountains were behind him and the Cimarron River was ahead. He hadn't seen a human since leaving Uncle Amos's.

Twice he jumped small bunches of antelope on the eastern Colorado prairie. The pronghorn animals watched him come, then ran away, skimming easily over the sagebrush, their white rumps shining in the afternoon sun. A characteristic of antelope was they'd try to cross in front of whatever started them running. These animals were on Bailey's left but they crossed to his right, then circled back behind him and went to where they'd started from. No horse could catch them.

Thinking about that brought a grin to Bailey's face. He'd owned a horse that could catch them. It was Booger Bay, the horse he'd traded at Arroyo Hondo. Of course, he had to admit to himself, if an antelope had a fair start, it'd leave a horse choking on the dust. But on a bet, with four horsemen watching, he'd sneaked up on a herd of antelope in Texas one day, gotten as close to them as he could before they saw him, then socked spurs to the bay and taken off after them.

The antelope could outrun any animal in North America. But they were a little slow getting started, and the horse was right in the middle of them before they even knew it. Ace hadn't tried to catch an antelope; he only wanted to prove that his horse could do it—and win a bet.

And thinking of the horse reminded him of why he'd had to leave Las Vegas in a hurry. It was over a horse race.

Ace had been in Las Vegas only two days. A horse track on the west side was what had brought him there. A lot of races were run on that track, he'd been told. He was drinking in a saloon when he mentioned that he had a running horse, a sprinter, that kept him in drinking money. It didn't take long to attract a challenge.

The fat man, chewing on a stub of a cigar, stepped up beside him. "So you've got a fast horse, eh?"

"Yup."

"Where you keepin' 'im?"

"In that livery barn across town."

"Let's go have a look-see."

"You interested in a race?"

"I might be."

Ace studied the round red face. The man talked like a lawman looking for a stolen horse, but he had no badge showing. No gun either. And Ace had come by the horse honestly, paying with cash and two other horses.

He said, "My name's Bailey," and waited for the other man to introduce himself.

"Hankins is my name. Ever'body calls me Hank."

"You got some running horses?"

A small crowd had gathered around the two men, listening intently, their eyes going from one face to the other.

"I happen to own the fastest hunk of horseflesh on four legs. She can eat up a half mile before you can say her name."

With a grin, Ace had to ask, "What's her name?"

"Booger Baby."

At that, Ace laughed out loud. "You won't believe it. I call my gelding Booger Bay."

"Haw. Now ain't that a coincidence."

"Yeah." Then Ace turned sober. "But I'll tell you, my horse is no half-miler. He's a sprinter. If you want to see him, let's go."

The crowd followed them outside, hanging back,

watching to see what was going to happen. But one man stepped up alongside the fat man, keeping pace with him, and Ace didn't like his looks. He was a tough, a gunslinger. His walnut-handled six-gun was cradled in a low tied-down holster, ready for a fast draw. He wore a cattleman's wide-brimmed hat on top and low-heeled mule ear boots at the bottom. Under the hat was a dark face with high cheekbones, a crooked nose, and a small, thin mouth.

Hankins was unarmed, but he had a well-armed friend.

At the barn, the crowd waited outside until Ace led the bay out and walked him in a circle. The horse was chunky, short in the back and legs, wide in the withers, with powerful muscles in the hindquarters.

"You say he can run?" Hankins asked.

"Nothing can catch him for two hundred yards. You want a race?"

"My mare'll leave him at the starting line."

"I hear you talking, but money talks louder. Go get your horse."

"I already sent for her. There's a mile track over yonder. Who's gonna ride your horse?"

"Well . . ." Ace pondered the question. "I'll ride him myself. I don't know anybody else." He grinned, "It's a cinch you ain't gonna ride your mare."

"Naw. I got a rider."

"I know where that racetrack is. I'll meet you there."

"How much money you planning on betting?"

"I've got a hundred and fifty on me."

"That's all you got?"

"Yup."

The fat man studied the ground a moment, then, "Oh well, that's better than nothing. My partner here can hold the money."

"Your partner?" Again Ace's eyes went over the gunslinger.

"That's right. You know somebody else that will hold it?"

"Naw," Ace said. "Naw, I'm a stranger here."

He knew then what he was getting into. But it didn't worry him. It didn't worry Ace Bailey one damned little bit.

Eighteen

"All right," Hankins said. I'll see you over at the track in twenty minutes."

"Make it thirty. I've got some business to take care of." Ace saddled the horse, kept the cinch loose enough that he could slide a finger between it and the animal's belly, then mounted and rode to the two-story adobe hotel, where he packed his saddlebags and rolled up his blankets. From there he went back to the livery barn and cached his belongings behind a haystack.

The racetrack, a flat length of land scraped clear of grass and rocks, lay a short distance north of the livery barn. Someone had paced the distances and marked them with stakes, a quarter mile, a half mile, three-quarters of a mile, and a mile.

An even bigger crowd had gathered. Excitement was in the air. All heads turned when someone yelled, "Hyar she comes." The gunslinger was leading the mare, a beautiful well-groomed sorrel. As soon as Ace saw her, he knew he was in for a race. She wore a saddle that wasn't much more than a cinch, a pair of stirrup straps, and iron stirrups. A small, thin Mexican boy of about fifteen walked alongside her. He weighed about eighty pounds.

The fat man pushed his way through the crowd. A fresh cigar stuck out of one side of his mouth. His red face was even redder than before. "A half mile? A quarter?"

"Two hundred yards," Ace said.

"Two hundred yards? What kind of race is that? Hell, I can pee that far."

The crowd haw-hawed.

"Two hundred yards."

"Well now, goddamn it, that's no race. No sir. If a horse can't run further than that, he ain't a runnin' horse."

"I told you he's a sprinter."

"Aw shit." Hankins turned to the crowd. "Ever see a horse race of only two hundred yards? This feller is trying to back out."

The crowd grumbled.

"Listen," Ace said, "I told you right from the beginning my horse is a sprinter. That means two hundred yards."

A tall, thin man in baggy wool pants and a bill cap came out of the crowd. "Let me pace off two hunnert yards and see how far it is." Without waiting, he stepped up to a line that had been drawn across the strip with a stick, then began walking with long steps and counting. When he had counted to two hundred, he stopped and looked back. "Right here," he yelled.

"Shit," said the fat man, "that ain't no race."

Bailey said, "Over in Texas most races are two hundred yards. They run horses on Sundays that pull plows on weekdays. That mare of yours is purty, but she couldn't pull your hat off. Do you want to race or don't you?"

"Pull plows, you say? You telling us that horse of yours is a plow horse?"

"He's worked in harness." Ace ran his right hand over the horse's left shoulder. "There's still some collar marks on him."

"Shit, ain't no plow horse can outrun my mare. Put up your money."

Ace handed all his money, folded, to the fat man, who handed it to the gunslinger. "I don't see any of your money," Ace said. The fat man lifted a cowhide wallet out of a hip pocket, removed a thick sheaf of bills, and

130

counted one hundred and fifty dollars. The gunslinger took it and folded it with Bailey's money, then put it all in a shirt pocket. A thin grin spread across his mouth, showing brown, crooked teeth.

"All right," Hankins said. "All right, now. I'm goin' down to that two-hundred yard mark. Wait 'til I give you a signal." He turned and walked. Most of the crowd followed. Ace once again checked the cinch on the bay, making sure it wasn't tight. A tight cinch could discourage a horse from running its best. He mounted.

The gunslinger helped the boy onto the mare's back. Having ridden races before, the boy got a fistful of mane in his right hand, knowing he would need something to hang on to. The mare pranced, slobbering on the mild snaffle bit. Ace's Booger Bay was calm until he urged it up close to the line drawn across the track, then it knew it was in for a race.

Good. It had to be a little nervous to be ready. It pulled on the bit but didn't fight its head. Ace held it back until the fat man yelled and waved his arms, then let it dance its way to the line.

"I'll shoot to start," the gunslinger said, drawing what looked to Ace to be a Smith and Wesson .45.

The two horses were on the line. The mare was nervous. She danced across the line, and had to be turned around and brought back. Ace squeezed with his lower legs to get Booger Bay's hind feet under him.

"Ready?

Ace nodded. The boy nodded. The gun fired.

Booger Bay jumped into a dead run so fast that Ace had to hang on to the saddle horn to keep his balance. Hooves pounding, nostrils flared, the two horses ran. At fifty yards Booger Bay was two lengths ahead.

The crowd was quiet, not believing their favorite racehorse was behind.

"Sic 'em, pardner," Ace whispered. "Sic 'em." Booger Bay's ears were laid back. Every muscle in his body was straining to hold the lead.

But the mare was gaining.

Now the crowd was yelling, cheering. At one hundred and twenty yards the lead was cut to one length.

"Keep on, pardner," Ace whispered. "Only a little farther."

The mare was still gaining. The crowd was wild.

At one hundred eighty yards Booger Bay was ahead by half a length. Then by a head. Then by half a head.

Then they crossed the finish line.

A loud "O-o-oh" came from the spectators. Ace let the horse slow gradually until it was walking, sides heaving, nostrils flared. "Atta boy, atta boy."

Deliberately, he walked the animal in a big circle until its breathing was back to normal and it was calm again. While he rode, he planned his escape. The haystack where he'd stashed his belongings was nearby; the road going west out of town was nearby. He saw no one with a lawman's badge. The only horses anywhere near were the two racehorses.

"I hope your running is over now," Ace said to Booger Bay, "but we'd better be ready."

He rode back to the crowd and stepped down. The fat man was holding his mare by the reins. His round face was the color of a prairie sunset. His cigar was almost chewed in two. Ace stepped up to the gunslinger.

"I'll take the money," he said.

The gunslinger looked over at the fat man.

"Oh no, you won't," the fat man bellowed. "That wasn't no horse race. Another ten yards and my mare would've won. I ain't payin' off on that kind of a race."

Shaking his head sadly, Ace drawled, "Well now, two hundred yards is what you agreed on, and it was a fair race." That tingling started in his legs and began working its way up.

"Besides," Hankins bellowed, "I ain't so sure your horse was ahead. Ever'body seen my mare catch up to him. I say it was a dead heat."

Shaking his head again, Ace said, "Naw. Everybody

here knows my horse was ahead by a nose. In a horse race, an inch is as good as a mile."

"Another ten yards and my mare would have won."

"That could be, but it wasn't. You lost. Pay up."

Hankins's face was purple now. "No, by God, I won't."

The crowd was looking back and forth from one man to the other.

Here it was.

A half smile appeared on Bailey's face. He stood in front of the gunslinger.

He said, "My name is Ace Bailey. You gonna give me the money?"

"Ace Bailey, huh?" A sneer appeared on the gunslinger's face.

The spectators were quiet, until someone whispered, "That there's Ace Bailey."

Quiet.

Ace said, "Hand it over."

Standing spraddle-legged, his right hand hovering over his gun butt, the gunslinger sneered, "Try and get it, Mr. Bailey."

A split second later he was falling. The loud POP from the .38 was ringing in everyone's ears.

While the dying man's legs twitched, Ace bent over him, took the folded sheaf of bills from his shirt pocket, and stuffed it into his own pocket. He holstered the Colt and stepped into Booger Bay's saddle. Hankins's mouth was open and spittle was running down his chin. Ace gave the crowd one glance.

"Adios," he said softly.

There was a sheriff in Las Vegas. Ace had seen him, noted that he looked capable, heard his name was Ackley, then dismissed him from his mind. Las Vegas seemed to be a peaceful town, and the sheriff didn't feel it necessary to keep an eye on everyone and everything. But Ace knew the lawman would gather some men and come after him.

133

He kept his horse at a slow lope, the saddlebags and blanket roll bouncing on the front of the saddle. On the other side of a low hill, four miles from town, he stopped, dismounted, and walked back to the crest. No one in sight. Not yet. There would be.

After tying the saddlebags and blankets behind the cantle, he mounted again and kept the horse at a mixed gait—trot a mile, lope a mile. It would soon be dark.

He spent the night in the Sangre de Cristos, letting the horse graze on the end of a thirty-foot rope. The smart thing to do, he knew, was to keep his saddle on the horse and be ready to ride. But the horse could rest better unsaddled. And after all, Booger Bay had just won him a hundred and fifty dollars.

While the horse grazed, Ace walked back a ways, over a low ridge, through a thick growth of juniper and cedar, and saw them. They were on his trail three or four miles away, but were camped with a cooking fire for the night, not being able to follow in the dark. At first light he was on his way again.

He skirted Santa Fe and rode north, where he picked up the Rio Grande. It occurred to him that the death of the gunslinger was no big loss to the town, and maybe the sheriff wouldn't try too hard to catch him. Unless fat Hankins had some political pull and could give the lawman a hard time. He had no way of knowing. He had to keep riding.

But Ace Bailey wasn't going to run a horse to death. Only mean sons of bitches did that. No sir, he'd rather take a stand and shoot it out with a posse.

If he'd had to, that's what he would have done.

Heat waves shimmered over the rolling hills of southeastern Colorado. The black horse traveled on at a slow, steady trot. What, Ace wondered, had become of Booger Bay? Who owned him now? Was the new owner treating him right?

134

Silently, he vowed that one day he'd find the horse and buy him back.

But not now. Now he was headed for home and more trouble. Soon he would be there.

Nineteen

A full moon shone like a bull's-eye lantern as Ace urged the black horse into the Cimarron River. "We'll be there in another hour," he promised. The horse splashed in water up to its belly. The river was quicksandy in places, but Ace knew this part of the country well. He knew where to cross.

There was no man-made light anywhere as he approached his childhood home. He rode halfway around the house and barn, picked out the harness team in a pen, and heard hogs grunting. Then he rode up to the kitchen door.

"Mom," he said quietly. Then louder, "Mom. Mother."

He was getting worried and was about to shout, when his mother said, "Who is it? Who's out there?"

"It's me, Mom. Alvin."

A lamp was lighted in the kitchen. It illuminated the window. It illuminated the doorway when Mrs. Bailey opened it and stood there in her old, worn plaid robe. "Alvin?"

In a second he was on the ground and had his arms wrapped around his mother. He hugged her tightly as she sobbed tears of relief, happiness, and sadness.

Finally, she said, "Come in the house, Alvin. Ain't nobody here but me."

"Is there horse feed in the barn?"

"Some. Take a lantern."

He didn't light the lantern until he was inside the barn. Then, his horse unsaddled and fed, he walked in the moonlight back to the house.

"They ain't come around lookin' for you lately," Mrs. Bailey said.

"How long has Pop been in jail?"

"Over a week now. But maybe they'll haveta let 'im go purty soon. Are you hungry? I can fire up the stove."

"Naw. Not now. How come they might have to let him go?"

"They're gettin' up a petition. A lot of folks in Stockwell County don't like that sheriff, and they want the county board to call an election so they can git rid of 'im."

"Who's carrying the petition?"

"Mr. Garrison. He's on the county board, and he owns the mercantile."

"Does he know Pop is innocent?"

Mrs. Bailey dropped heavily into a kitchen chair while Ace stood with his back against the door. "Well, I don't think he's convinced of that, but he don't like Sheriff Petersen and his hoodlums."

"When did he start carrying the petition?"

"'Bout a week ago."

Looking at the floor and shaking his head, Ace muttered, "Damn," then hurriedly changed it to "Durn." He made certain the door was latched, then sat in another wooden chair. "That'll take too long. He has to get a lot of folks to sign it and he has to take it to the board and the board has to call an election, and there has to be an election, and . . . aw, durn it." After a moment of silence, he asked, "How is Pop?"

"He don't look good."

"I've got to get him out of there."

A long sigh came from Mrs. Bailey. Her wrinkled, work-worn face was twisted with worry. "You cain't. There's too many of 'em. And even if you did shoot 'em

137

all and bust your pop out of jail, they'd just arrest 'im again."

"What if the sheriff was dead?"

"The board would appoint somebody else and the reverend would be put back in jail 'til a trial and all."

Ace's hands were clenched into fists. "Damn. Durn."

"We got this farm and we ain't young and we cain't run like you can."

"When's the trial?"

"We don't know yet. The judge is busy ever'where else. Besides, Mr. Garrison said most folks think he gave you a gun so you could shoot that deputy and get out of jail."

"He didn't."

"I know it and you know it, but nobody knows who else coulda done it."

"I could testify at his trial."

"And then you'd be arrested again."

"Yeah, and I'd have to name Marybelle Stewart, and she'd be in trouble, and maybe nobody would believe me, and . . . aw, durn it."

"All we can do is pray, Alvin. That's what Mr. Bailey said."

Ace's fists were still clenched. "There's got to be something else we can do."

They were silent a long moment, Bailey's brow wrinkled in thought. Then he asked, "There was a lot of cattle stealing going on when Jim was arrested. Is it still going on?"

"That's what Mr. Garrison said. Some prime beefs was stole up in Colorada just a few days ago."

"You said Jim was working for a rancher over in Texas and quit when he found out his boss was buying stolen cattle. What's the rancher's name?"

"George Alberts."

"Where's his ranch?"

"Jim said it was north of Animas. That's just across the Texas border. Why?"

138

"I've been studying on it, and so have some other folks. How does Sheriff Petersen pay those deputies?"

"Mr. Garrison is puzzled about that, too."

"He's not honest, we all know that."

"Mr. Garrison said a lot of folks suspicion it, but nobody can prove it. Why?"

Another pause in the conversation, then Ace said, "I don't get it. Sheriff Petersen is getting money from somewhere, and a lot of folks know it. How come they let him stay this long?"

"I reckon it's like Mr. Garrison said. Before Sheriff Petersen was elected, there was a shootin' at least once a week in Stockwell, and there was a lot of drinkin' and carousin' and fightin'. Sheriff Petersen and his deputies put a stop to that. The town folks and merchants appreciate it, and most won't sign the petition."

"It doesn't matter to the town folks that the ranchers and farmers are being robbed?"

"I reckon not."

"What if folks knew Petersen is a liar and thief? What would they do?"

"Git rid of 'im, I reckon. Ever'body'd sign the petition."

"Would they let Pop out of jail?"

"They prob'ly would."

"Everybody knows Pop wouldn't run."

"Maybe," Mrs. Bailey said thoughtfully, "if folks knew the shurff was a thief hisself, they'd run 'im off and let the reverend out of jail 'til the trial."

"And if that happened, maybe there wouldn't even be a trial."

"Prob'ly not."

"Well," Ace said, brow still wrinkled in thought, "that settles it, then."

"What're you gonna do, Alvin?"

"I think I'll ride down to Animas and have a palaver with George Alberts."

"You ain't gonna shoot nobody, are you?"

139

"I'm not planning to," Ace said. "But then I never planned to—until I met Sheriff Petersen."

He stayed at home the next day, going outside only long enough to feed and water his horse. He could see at a glance that the corn crop was ruined and the maize wasn't going to mature. The Baileys would have no feed to sell, and barely enough for the harness team and the milk cow. While Pop is praying, he muttered under his breath, he'd better pray for an easy winter. Shortly after dark he kissed his mother on the cheek and rode away, angling south by southeast. He'd been through the Texas town of Animas before and he remembered it as a quiet cattle town.

He crossed Carrizo Creek and Corrumpa Creek and stayed to the east of Rabbit Ear Mountain, then he believed he was in Texas. The sun was about to show itself over the Texas plains when he found a grassy swale and dismounted.

"We'll rest til the flies get to eating on us," he said to the horse. It wasn't long. The higher the sun climbed, the higher the temperature rose and the worse the flies became. He resaddled the black horse and rode out of the swale. When he came to a wagon road going northwest, Ace figured it was the road from Animas to Clayton, Territory of New Mexico, and he reined up. Animas was about five miles east. He would rather stay out of the town, but he needed directions to George Alberts's ranch. The best thing to do, he decided, was to wait by the road until he saw a wagon coming, then mount up and pretend he was going to Animas to ask directions. Maybe whoever was in the wagon would know the way.

With irony, he thought about how much easier it was to travel on the plains, but how much hotter and how little shade there was. It must have been a hundred degrees and there was not a tree in sight. Ace and the horse both needed water. He sat on the ground and waited. Flies kept him busy as he brushed them off his

140

arms and face, and they kept the horse shaking its head and stomping its feet. It was nearly noon before he saw a wagon coming from the east. He mounted and rode slowly to meet it.

As it drew closer he saw it was a light wagon, pulled by two horses that probably didn't weigh more than a thousand pounds each. A man wearing a broad-brimmed hat and a woman wearing a poke bonnet sat on the spring seat. Two boys, both under ten, sat on sacks of grain next to a wooden barrel in the back.

When Ace raised his hand, the man "Whoaed" the team.

"Howdy, folks." Ace smiled.

"How do."

"Hot day."

"Shore is." The man had a stern face, smooth shaven. He wore overalls with suspenders. The woman was thin, stringy. Her face reflected a lifetime of hard labor.

"I'm looking for a gentleman name of Alberts, George Alberts, and I think his ranch is somewhere this side of Animas, but I don't know where. Y'all wouldn't happen to know, would you?"

"Yup." The man pointed a crooked finger northeast. "See that there butte?"

Ace could barely see it through the heat waves, but he made out a long, low hill that seemed to rise out of the prairie, then end abruptly. "Yessir, I see it."

"You go around the end of it and on the other side is a crik. The Alberts's Mill Iron Ranch is right there. There's nothin' else to see so you can't miss it."

"I'm sure obliged to you folks. You saved me some riding."

"It ain't far, but I reckon you could use a drink of water. We got a barrel back here. Ain't got enough for your horse, but like I said, it ain't far."

"I'd sure appreciate it."

"Daniel, give the traveler a drink."

141

A boy with a sheaf of sun-bleached hair sticking out from under a bill cap stood, pried the lid off a wooden barrel, reached a hand in, and pulled out a tin dipper of water. Ace edged his horse close enough to reach without getting down. He drank, said "Much obliged," then turned the black horse south.

Distances were deceiving, and it took an hour to get to the end of the butte and another half hour to get around to the other side. There was a creek, a line of brush, tall weeds, and a few stunted trees. And there was a ranch — a long, low house made of lumber, a barn, a few wooden corrals. A heavy freight wagon was parked near the barn and beyond it was a buggy with a roof. In front of the barn was a man with a rifle.

Ace rode forward slowly, eyes busy. Another man came out of the barn, then another man on horseback came from around the barn. The three watched him come. No cattle were in sight, but that wasn't unusual on a Texas-sized ranch.

"Howdy," Ace said when he was within earshot.

No answer. The three didn't take their eyes off him.

"I'm looking for a gentleman name of Alberts, George Alberts."

"Who might you be?" The man who asked was average in height and weight, with a bushy brown beard and squinty eyes. He wore a straw hat almost as big as the ones the Mexicans wore. He also wore bullhide batwing chaps. At first glance Ace wondered why, as hot as it was and with no brush in sight, he wore the chaps.

Now Ace had to think fast. If he gave his name, they would connect him with Jim Bailey. He should have had this all figured out before he got here. "My name is . . . uh . . . Grant. Bill Grant." He'd met a Bill Grant in Dodge City once.

"Where you from?"

"Uh . . . down in the Big Bend country." Damn, he knew as soon as he said it that it wouldn't do. Down

142

there riders had to wear chaps no matter how hot it was.

"Whatta you want?"

"A job."

"Doin' what?"

"Cowboying. Anything."

Nobody spoke for a long moment. The three continued to study him, from the weathered sweat-stained hat, to the pearl-handled .38, to the Texas spurs. Especially the .38 in its low holster.

"You ain't with the laws, are you?"

"The laws?" Ace cracked a wry grin. "They're the last ones I'd be with."

"You runnin' from the law?"

"Well, I sure ain't running very fast."

"Ever been up to Dodge?"

"Yep, I have. Been up the trail twice."

"Who for?"

"My brother and me, and once for the Circle B outfit out of Grand Prairie."

"Well, we're puttin' together a trail herd. We're holdin' 'em over yonder four . . . five miles and slappin' a road brand on 'em. We can use another hand. Buck twenty-five a day and chuck. You got a bed?"

"Not much of one, but it'll do."

One of the other men spoke next: "I got a couple blankets and a tarp I'll sell you if you got any money."

"I've got a few bucks."

"Well," the bearded one said, "we just et and there ain't nothing left here. We'll eat again tonight at the wagon. You can get a drink for yourself and your horse over there at the creek."

"I take it you are George Alberts."

"I am." George Alberts squinted at Ace, at the western horizon, at the butte, then back at Ace. He grinned a weak grin, showing broken brown teeth inside the bushy beard. "And you'd better be who you say you are."

143

Twenty

They rode northwest at a trot, nobody speaking. While they rode Ace sneaked glances at the men. They were a hard bunch. Cowboys, for sure, from the way they sat their horses. But they carried their six-guns in low holsters, and their eyes were constantly studying the horizon with a guarded look. Alberts carried a six-gun and a rifle. When Ace took a second look at the batwing chaps, he saw why Alberts wore them: Cartridge loops had been sewn just below the belt, and they held at least twenty cartridges.

He heard the cattle long before he saw them, and he could tell from the bawling there were mother cows among them. Ahead was a line of stunted oak trees, thick buck brush, and tall weeds. Ace guessed it was Carrizo Creek. The country beyond was rolling hills with a few dry shallow arroyos. The grass had been overgrazed.

They crossed the creek at a place where it was wide but not deep, and reined up.

"We'll cut out the wet stuff and kick 'em across the creek," Alberts said to the riders. "Grant, you can hold the cut 'til we get 'em mothered up."

The cattle were being held in a bunch by five cowboys. Away off to the north was the remuda, grazing on brown bunch grass. A covered chuck wagon was parked farther down the creek. Ace guessed there were about fifteen hundred cattle, and from where he was he couldn't see any fresh brands.

"I could use another horse," he said to Alberts. "This old pony has traveled a long ways."

Alberts gave the black horse a quick look and said, "He don't 'pear to be too bad off, and we ain't gonna run the remuda in this time of day. You can hold the cut right here."

Ace hung back and watched. The three riders joined the five with the herd, each man taking a position. Alberts rode slowly into the herd and began cutting out the cows and calves. His sorrel horse had obviously cut cattle before, but it wasn't the best cutting horse Ace had ever seen.

When Alberts had a cow or calf out of the herd and headed his way, Ace got in behind it and drove it on to the creek. Alberts rode back into the herd after another. The calves were separated from their mothers and were hard to handle. One, a late summer calf, refused to join the others at the creek and almost ran under Ace's horse getting back to the herd. Alberts rode out, face red around the bushy beard.

"Goddamn it, you said you was a cowboy. Can't you hang on to a little ol' suckin' calf?"

"What the hell do you expect me to do?" Ace said. "Pick him up and carry him?"

"Ain't you got a goddamn rope?"

"Yeah, then what? Drag him back? And what'll the rest of them do in the meantime?"

"Well, goddamn it, when I cut out a cow brute, I want it to stay out. If you can't do it, I'll get somebody else."

He was being unreasonable. Ace knew from hard experience that when a calf that small wanted to go back, nobody on a horse could stop it. It would run right under a horse. The only way was to rope and tie it, and while he was doing that the other cattle would scatter. The fact was there were too many calves for one man to handle. Quit, Ace said to himself. Tell this son of a bitch where to go and then send him there.

Naw. Hold your temper, Ace Bailey. You came here to learn something about some cattle rustling, so just hold your water and keep quiet. He turned the black horse around and started gathering the cows that had been cut out.

Soon he had about fifty cows and almost that many calves gathered next to the creek. They were bawling and not easy to hold. All were determined to go back to wherever they'd come from. The black horse was working hard. All wore the Mill Iron brand.

When Alberts rode out of the herd without a cow in front of him, he gave an arm signal and two cowboys rode up to him. "Let's let 'em mother up and push 'em across the water," he said.

They held the cows and calves in a loose bunch until mothers and calves found one another and the bawling had ceased. Calves were butting the cows' flanks, sucking and slobbering.

Finally, about sundown, Ace got to ride with the other men to the main herd. Most of the brands were grown over with hair and hard to read, but after a careful study, Ace decided there wasn't a Mill Iron among them.

After chuck, he was told he'd better be ready for night guard. The chuck was good: fresh-butchered beef, beans, and baking soda biscuits. A cowboy tried to trade him out of his pearl-handled .38, then tried to hoo-raw him into a shooting match. Ace didn't want to show his skill with the gun and begged off, saying he had no ammunition to spare.

Most men who were not horseback rolled up in their beds. Two others stayed up and smoked hand-rolled cigarettes, but spoke very little. There was no story-telling nor joking, no talk of other cow outfits, horses, or other places. Nobody asked Ace where he was from or where he'd worked before. Nobody asked anybody anything.

A strange crew, Ace thought. Outlaws, for sure.

The next ten days was all hard work. The dry cattle were driven five miles east over a long, low hill to a big pen built of rough-sawn planks. Branding began. Two men who were handy with catch ropes headed and heeled the cattle one at a time. Still, it took another man on foot to push a steer over on its right side, pull its tail up between its legs, and sit with his knees on its back pulling on its tail, to hold it still. That was Ace's job. He saw four brands other than the Mill Iron. There were about forty long yearlings wearing a Double A, and there were the Flying U, the EZ, and the Frying Pan. The cattle had almost every earmark there was: the overbit, underbit, overslope, underslope, swallow fork. Within two weeks, they all wore a fresh Mill Iron brand. It was hard work, and the crew was shorthanded.

Ace kept quiet, asking no questions. No answers were needed. He knew how it worked. A herd was put together from four or five different cow outfits, and every brute in the herd had to have a fresh road brand. Any lawman who asked about an old brand was addressed by one of the crew who claimed to represent that brand. Every different brand had a rep among the crew. Signatures could be forged on bills of sale.

One of the cowboys let it slip during a smoking session after chuck. "I'm the EZ," he said matter-of-factly. "Up in Colorada."

"Where in Colorado?" Ace asked, trying to sound only mildly interested.

"Why, it's just across the border, east of Trinidad."

"Somewhere near the Denver and Rio Grande Railroad?"

"Yeah, we take in a lot of country between the railroad and the Cimarron."

The man was lying. The railroad that went from east to west across southern Colorado was the Atchison, Topeka and Santa Fe.

"Well," Ace said, still trying to sound as if he were making casual conversation, "I reckon it's cheaper to trail cattle to Dodge than to ship them by rail."

"Cheaper, and if there ain't been too many up the trail ahead of us, these beefs can put on some weight along the way."

Sure, sure, Ace thought, but he said no more. Instead he went to catch his night horse. So the cattle were stolen. He had known that the first day he'd worked for the outfit. But after two weeks, he hadn't found a way to tie the sheriff of Stockwell County to cattle stealing.

It was two days later that he saw three of the deputies from Stockwell.

They were driving about thirty-five prime beeves ahead of them, coming from the west. Ace kept his head down, and he was far enough away that he doubted they'd recognized him. But they would.

It was dusk, and the crew had just branded the last steer. Alberts saw the deputies coming, and he cursed. "Now what in hell? Goddamn it, how many beefs do they think we can handle? Shit, I wanted to get this goddamn herd movin' first thing in the mornin'. Now we got more to brand. Shit, they better be willin' to help."

Ace had been riding company horses, and he had one, a blue roan with a long back, saddled and hobbled near the branding pen. While the three deputies were still a hundred yards away, he casually walked over to the chuck wagon, tore two pages out of the cook's Sears and Roebuck catalog, and walked away toward the horse. No one paid him any attention, thinking he was going somewhere to relieve himself. Horseback, he started toward the herd, looked back to see Alberts greeting the three deputies, then turned the horse south.

148

That was when the shouting started. And the shooting. Nothing to do but ride for it. "Come on, pardner," he said to the blue roan, "we're in for a horse race." He had enough of a head start that it would take a lucky shot from a pistol to hit him or the horse, but if Alberts got down and took careful aim with that rifle of his, Ace could be put afoot. He half turned in the saddle and fired two shots from the .38, hoping to slow them down. It worked for a few seconds. There were four riders after him, and when they saw they were being shot at, they stopped. But only for a few seconds.

Ace heard a rifle crack, but Alberts was horseback and his aim was bad. "Do your damnedest, feller," Ace said to the horse. "You're a bigger target than I am. Run for your life."

He'd had it planned since the first day with the outfit. If a deputy from Stockwell showed up with stolen cattle, he'd try to take him back there and make him confess. If there was no way to do that, he'd ride for Animas. And it was unlikely he could do that. There had to be a sheriff or marshal or some kind of lawman in Animas.

The rifle cracked again. He glanced back. Alberts was on the ground, kneeling, taking aim. Ace was on the open prairie but the country was dotted with sagebrush, yucca, and bunch grass, and the horse had to be always dodging and jumping. That made it a poor target for anyone but a damned good rifleman. When the rifle fired again, Ace felt the heat of the bullet as it went past his head.

The race went on. Hooves pounding, nostrils flared, the blue roan was doing its best, but it was tiring. Another glance back showed Ace the four were still after him. Either they were going to have to give up soon or he was going to have to bail off and shoot it out. If there were an arroyo, a tree, or anything to take cover behind, that's what he'd do. There was nothing.

149

But just ahead was a wagon road and it led in the direction of Animas. "Keep going, pard," Ace pleaded. "Not much farther."

Another rifle shot, and again the lead bullet sang a deadly song past Ace's ear. Every time old Alberts gets down to take aim, we get farther ahead, Ace thought. But here in the wagon tracks the blue roan didn't have to dodge and jump, and was a better target.

When Ace twisted in the saddle and looked back again, one man who was better mounted was ahead of the others, firing a six-gun. Damned if he didn't almost get lucky. A lead slug jerked at Ace's shirt collar and stung the side of his neck.

"Sonofabitch," Ace muttered. He wiped the side of his neck with his right hand and saw blood. "If we can get far enough away from the others, I'll take that sonofabitch on." But when he looked back, the others were still coming.

Now it was turning dark. That was good. He could hide in the dark. In fact, he had a whole damned prairie to hide in. But the blue roan wasn't going to last until dark. Ahead, far ahead, was the town. Too damned far. The horse was staggering.

Desperate, Ace took a long look around and saw what he hoped to see. An arroyo. A real, good old New Mexico-type arroyo. It was off to his right a hundred yards. He tried to turn the horse in that direction, but the animal was too beat to respond. Ace stepped off on the run, stumbled, regained his balance, and ran.

While he ran, Alberts fired at him with the rifle, and bullets whistled by him. The bullets made him so uncomfortable that Ace hit the ground on his belly and slid headfirst into the arroyo. It was only four feet deep and sandy. But by staying low, Ace was out of danger — for the moment. From a squatting position, he fired two more shots to let his pursuers know he was plenty able to

150

fight back, then looked for the blue roan. The horse had stopped and was standing with its head down, sides heaving.

"Atta boy. You'll live," Ace muttered.

Then a bullet kicked dirt in his face, and he saw that the four were on foot now, spread out and coming toward him, shooting as they advanced.

Twenty-one

With the nimble fingers of a card player, Ace Bailey reloaded the Colt .38 and looked for someone to shoot at. Alberts. He was reloading that rifle. No time to aim, just point and shoot. Ace saw his shot poke a hole in Alberts's bullhide batwing chaps. A bullet slammed into the ground only inches from Ace's face. He snapped a shot at the closest man. The man clutched his side and fell backward. Lead was smacking into the ground all around Ace's head, and he ducked. Then he cursed himself.

Stay down, you dumb farmer, and they'll just walk up and pump you full of lead. Shoot.

He raised up and fired, ducked, raised up and fired again. Time to move, he told himself. They're zeroed in on me now. Keeping low, Ace ran to his left twenty feet, raised up, and fired at the closest man. Out of the corner of his eye, he saw a man slide into the arroyo at the spot he'd just vacated. He fired. The man dropped his gun and pitched facedown into the bottom of the arroyo. That's two down, Ace thought. The other two will be more careful.

But the .38 was empty. Goddamn.

Kneeling, he barely had time to punch out the empties and shove a live round into the cylinder, when he heard footsteps above him. Quickly, he slammed the cylinder home and looked up, ready for one shot. But no one showed.

Alberts cursed, "Goddamn. That sonofabitch is down

152

in there like a goddamned gopher. Go in and git 'im."

"You go git 'im, goddamnit. You're the one that hired 'im."

"Shit, if it wasn't so goddamned dark, I would, but hell, I can't see good enough."

From their voices, Ace figured they were right above him but were not willing to risk their lives by peering over the edge to look for him.

"Me neither."

"Goddamnit, we git to stumblin' around in the dark, we might shoot each other."

"Well, you're the boss. Whatta you wanta do?"

"Go back. He ain't the law. I went through all his stuff—his pockets and everything—while he was sleepin', and he ain't got a badge or paper of any kind. I'll bet he's got the law after 'im, and he ain't gonna blab."

"If that's so, why'd he run?"

"You seen them three comin' from the west with some beefs, didn't you? They're deputies from over in New Mexico Territory. I'll bet he recognized 'em, got scairt, and ran."

They were silent a moment, then the other man chuckled. "Well, he's either a lawman or a law dodger, and a lawman don't run from the law."

Another chuckle. "No, and I fair worked the shit out of 'im. No law dog's gonna work that hard."

There was the sound of footsteps going away. Ace could have raised up and shot them in the back, but he didn't. He just waited. "Whatta we gonna do with them corpses?"

"What the hell you think? Pack 'em to town and hand 'em to Sheriff Reuben?"

The footsteps and voices were soon out of hearing distance.

First thing he had to do, Ace decided, was to try to find the blue roan horse. When he climbed out of the arroyo, it was so dark he couldn't see anything at all. The

153

full moon that had guided him when he left home had run its course, and now there was no moon. He reloaded the Colt by feel and started walking in the direction of the road to town. He had to go into town. But Lord, he hated walking. A man walking into town would attract a lot of attention. And though he had a few dollars left from the wages Adam Potter had paid him, he didn't have enough to buy another horse and saddle.

Well hell, he said to himself, you can't stand out here on the prairie all night, either. Either walk to town, or walk in the other direction and hope to catch a ride on a wagon going somewhere.

He walked, stumbled over a jagged yucca, tripped when his feet hit a low spot, and walked some more. Then his feet told him he was on the wagon road, and he squatted and groped the ground with his hands. His feet had been correct. Listen.

Standing still, ears straining, Ace listened. Not a sound. Not even a night breeze. He could hear his heart beating.

The plan he'd worked out—in case he couldn't take a Stockwell deputy back with him—was to hunt up whatever officer of the law he could find in Animas and . . . But damnit, he hadn't planned on being afoot and walking into Animas in the dark.

Go in the opposite direction? Hell no. If he did, all the work he'd done in the past ten days, the information he'd gathered, would be for nothing. So walk.

Listen.

Was that a horse blowing through its nostrils, that fluttering sound horses make? Listen. Footsteps. Hooves? Yeah. And the faint creak of saddle leather. The blue roan was nearby.

The horse was a remuda horse, not plumb gentle, but if he could find it, maybe he could catch it. Find it, hell. It was so dark he couldn't find his ass with both hands. Listen.

154

The horse was off to his left somewhere but was invisible in the dark.

Looking up, Ace saw stars, dim ones. Looking ahead, he could barely see where the prairie met the sky.

But the sky was a shade lighter than the prairie, and Ace knew how to make use of that light. Riding night guard on a herd of cattle, hunting possums as a kid, had taught him. First, get as close to that horse as he could. Move slowly and listen. He moved, trying not to make a sound.

He was closer. Cropping, chewing sounds told him the horse was grazing. But horses had good night vision, and it had no doubt seen him. Would it keep away from him? There was no way in the world that a man on foot could catch a horse that didn't want to be caught. Talk to it.

"Whoa, pardner. I apologize for riding you so hard. They would have killed us if I hadn't. Whoa, now."

Ace believed he was closer, but still he couldn't see the horse. But if he could get the horse between him and the sky, he could see it in the dim skylight. Maybe. He dropped to his hands and knees, then lay down and looked in the direction he believed the horse to be. The skyline was visible, but nothing else was. Standing, Ace continued talking, "Whoa, feller. I'm harmless. I promise I won't run you that hard again." He moved fifty feet and dropped to the ground again. Still nothing. Listen.

The horse was moving. Now it stopped. It was no doubt watching him. Ace moved to a different position, talking softly. He lay on the ground. His eyes scanned the skyline.

He saw the horse. It was straight ahead, standing still. All right, seeing a man on his hands and knees might spook a horse. Stand up and walk toward him. Walk right up to him as if he were hobbled. Walk like there was no doubt you were going to catch him.

Talking softly, Ace walked. The horse snorted. He was

close. Careful. Don't walk up to his rear end. Where was his head? Ace squatted, got the horse in the skylight, stood, then went and took hold of the bridle reins.

"Boy, am I glad to find you. Wish I had some grain to feed you." He scratched the horse's neck, then groped for the cinch and latigo. The cinch was tight enough. A minute later he was mounted and heading the blue roan in the direction he believed the town to be.

Folks in Animas, Texas went to bed early, and only a few windows showed any light at all. Three horses were tied to a hitchrail in front of a wide, low building with illuminated windows. There was a sign over the door, but it was too dark to read, anyhow. Probably a saloon. A man stood just outside the door, smoking. A red glow appeared when he sucked on his cigarette. "Evenin'," Ace said, and heard a barely audible reply. On down the street was another wide building with a false front. Probably a mercantile. Dark.

Turning the horse around, Ace went back to the saloon. "I'm a stranger here," he said to the smoker. "Is there a livery barn?"

A man's voice answered from the dark. "Two blocks back and turn north. Old Abe's drunk, but you can leave your horse there."

"Obliged."

Abe was drunk, all right. He was sitting in a cubbyhole of an office with a bottle of bourbon on an overturned wooden crate used as a desk. A coal oil lamp emitted a smoky light. The building was a large one, and the smell of horses and manure left no doubt it was a barn.

The man named Abe was a dwarf hunchback whose head came from between his shoulders without a neck. He was old, with a ragged black hat pulled down to his eyes and a week's growth of dirty whiskers. One eye was only a slit.

"Sorry to bother you," Ace said, stepping inside the cubbyhole, "but I've got a horse that's tired and hungry."

The grotesque shape twisted toward him, and one eye took him in. A callused hand waved toward the black innards of the barn. Blurred speech told Ace to "find a shtall."

"Where do you keep the feed?"

The hand waved toward the insides of the barn again.

"Can I borrow a light?"

Again the hand waved.

Ace took the lantern and walked down a row of box stalls until he found an empty one. He went back and led the roan horse inside, pulled the saddle off, and put it in the stall. The horse had never seen the inside of a barn before, and it was snorty, but obedient. Then Ace went looking for feed. In another stall he found a pile of hay and a wooden barrel half full of whole oats.

Horse fed, he went back to the cubbyhole and put the lantern on the upturned wooden box. "How much do I owe you?"

"Fitty shents."

Ace put two quarters beside the lamp. The lamp was empty of fuel, and only the wick was burning now. Burning and smoking. It would soon go out. "Thanks. See you in the morning," Ace said.

Instead of going out to the street, he went to the pile of hay, flopped down on his back, and tried to sleep. Lord, he said to himself, if I looked like him, I'd stay drunk, too. Not until now did he again feel the stinging wound on the left side of his neck. He touched it with his fingers, decided it wasn't deep, and tried to ignore it. I hope folks who keep horses here know enough to do their own feeding. Surely, they do. Finally, he slept.

In the morning he led the blue roan to a tank of water and watched it suck the liquid up between its lips. With his fingers he again felt for the wound on his neck. Unbuttoning his shirt, he removed the garment and washed

157

the blood off the collar in the cold water of the stock tank. He washed his face and neck. Then he led the horse back to the stall and fed it. His own stomach grumbled, but instead of hunting for a cafe he went to the mercantile. There he bought a loaf of bread, some apple butter, three cans of beans, and a tin of sardines. He also talked a clerk out of an empty gunnysack.

Back at the barn, the hunchback had his arms folded on top of the wooden crate and his head in his arms. He snored, and he had wet his pants. Shaking his head sadly, Ace saddled the blue roan, tied the gunnysack to the saddle horn, and tied the horse to a hitchrail in back of the barn. I might be a while, he said to the horse, and he carried an armful of hay out to the hitchrail. Finish your breakfast. By then two other men had showed up to feed their horses. Both said "Mornin'," then went on about their business. A third man showed up and allowed, "One of these mornings we're gonna find Old Abe dead."

"Sure enough," a man said.

Ace went looking for the sheriff's office and hoped he wasn't too early. He was.

Animas County had a two-story courthouse made of bricks hauled from somewhere. The door was locked, and Ace had to wait until a man in a finger-length coat and a white shirt unlocked it. The sheriff's office, he was told, was on the second floor. Ace climbed the stone stairs and waited. A sign on a door at the head of the stairs read: JASPER REUBEN - SHERIFF ANIMAS COUNTY. It was after eight o'clock when Jasper Reuben showed up.

"You waiting for me?" he asked. The sheriff of Animas County was six feet two and thin, with a grey moustache and long grey sideburns. He wore a rancher's wide-brimmed hat and striped wool pants. A silver badge pinned to his shirt left no doubt as to who he was. That, and a big caliber pistol on his right hip.

"Yes sir, I am. "

After unlocking the door with a long key, the lawman said, "Come in." They both entered. Sheriff Reuben sat in a swivel chair at a new but scarred desk, tilted the chair back, and said, "What do you wanta see me about?" A gun rack behind the sheriff held a lever action rifle and a double-barreled shotgun. A door on the right was open, and jail bars were visible behind it. A pile of wanted posters lay on the desk. Beside the pile was a pair of handcuffs, open.

Ace stood with his back to the door, thumbs hooked inside his gunbelt. "Do you know who I am?"

"Why no, I don't believe . . ." Suddenly, the sheriff's eyes widened, and he stiffened in his chair. "Say, you're not? . . . Are you? . . ."

"Yep."

"Why, you're . . ." Reuben's hand moved toward his gun.

"Now, don't go and get yourself shot, Sheriff. You know damned well I can plug you right where you sit."

Twenty-two

Sheriff Jasper Reuben's hand stopped moving. "Well, what, uh? . . ."

"I've got news for you."

"News? What news?"

"Ever hear of a cattleman named Alberts?"

"Sure."

"He's buying stolen cattle."

"Whatta you mean?"

"He's got a herd of about fifteen hundred beeves ready to trail up to Dodge City. They're wearing at least four different brands as well as his own."

"So what? He's been trailing cattle to market for other cowmen for several years. He knows that trail better'n anybody."

"These cattle were stolen."

"Why do you say that?"

"I've been working for him. I know."

Sheriff Reuben's eyes studied the floor while he absorbed the news. Then he looked up. "What's your interest in this?"

Ace shifted his weight from one foot to the other. "I've got two problems. My pop's in jail in Stockwell, New Mexico for something he didn't do, and the sheriff and his deputies over there are thieves and killers. I've got to prove it on them and I've got to get my pop out of jail."

"Well now," the lawman studied the floor again, "I can't lope over there and put the whole outfit under arrest just on your say-so."

"Send some telegraphs. Send some riders to the laws in New Mexico and Colorado and the Panhandle. You'll find out a lot of cattle have been rustled. Then go out to Alberts' Mill Iron Ranch and you'll find about fifteen hundred of them."

Rubbing his jaw in thought, Reuben said, "We ain't got a telegraph here yet. I reckon I could find some riders to visit some of the sheriffs in other jurisdictions. But that'll take time."

"You've got time. They can't move that herd very fast."

"And I got only one deputy. How many hands are working that herd?"

Ace had to do some mental calculating. "Eleven, I believe. No . . . I shot two last night near an arroyo west of here. They were trying to kill me. And three of them are deputies from Stockwell County. I doubt they'll help move the herd. That leaves only six." Ace snorted. "Old Alberts is shorthanded. You can catch up easy."

"You say they tried to kill you? Is that a bullet track on the side of your neck?"

Fingering the wound with his left hand, Ace said, "Yeah. How does it look? Can you see it from there?"

"It don't look bad, but you ought to put something on it."

"It's a long way from my heart. Now, like I said, this is your chance to catch a bunch of rustlers and a lot of stolen cattle."

"Well . . ." Reuben scratched his jaw and studied the floor. "All I've got is your word for it and you're a . . . uh . . ."

"Wanted man." Ace finished the sentence for him. "But I'm not a thief and I'm not a liar. If you want to put a stop to some cattle rustling, here's your chance."

"Well, I . . ."

"What do you say? Are you gonna do it?"

Looking up, Reuben asked, "You said you want to prove the sheriff in Stockwell, New Mexico is a thief. How—if him and his deputies ain't with that herd—can you do that?"

"I'm gonna have to catch those deputies—at least one of them—and when you round up the rest of the bunch, some of them will talk. And they'll point out any of the deputies they happen to see."

"Then what?"

"Then I want you to send a rider to Stockwell with a note from you. Send it to a man named Garrison, who runs the mercantile there. He's on the county board. Tell Garrison what you'll learn from the deputies."

"Damn." Sheriff Reuben scowled at the floor, then scowled at Ace. "We're gonna have some ridin' to do."

"You've got your work cut out for you."

"Damn."

"Are you gonna do it?"

"Well . . . I'll send some riders out to the other jurisdictions. If what you said is true, I'll get some help. Some of the cattlemen who've been stolen from, they'll help. And I can deputize some men here in town."

"They're a tough bunch. I wouldn't go riding out there by myself if I was you."

"What are you gonna do? How're you gonna capture those deputies?"

"I'm gonna have to give that some thought," Ace said. "I'll leave now." He stepped over to the desk, picked up the handcuffs, and stuffed one cuff under his belt behind his back, leaving the other one dangling. "I'll borrow these."

"Listen, there's a back door and a back stairwell up here. Go out that way, will you? I don't want anybody to see you walking out of my office."

With a wry grin, Ace said, "That wouldn't do at all, would it? Not a-tall."

Sheriff Reuben made no move as Ace went through the door, past two empty jail cells, through another door, and down the back stairs. He didn't hurry. Walking like a man out for a morning stroll, he went to the livery barn, tightened the cinch on the blue roan horse, mounted, and rode out of town.

Five miles west of Animas, he dismounted and let the horse graze while he ate the tin of sardines and two thick slices of bread smeared with apple butter. "Won't take the place of hotcakes and bacon," he mused aloud, "but it'll do. Now what?"

The plan he had in mind was a vague one. Sitting on the ground, keeping an eye toward Animas, he mulled it over, trying to work out the details. He had to take at least one of the Stockwell deputies alive. How could he do that?

He couldn't just ride up to a crew of cowboys, especially a tough bunch like the Mill Iron, and kidnap one of them. Somehow he had to get one of the deputies alone. Could he catch one in the dark? Naw, he'd have to be damned lucky to do that. Think, he told himself.

His thoughts went instead to his dad. His mother had said he was doing poorly in jail. That was ten . . . twelve days ago. A man could die in that jail. Ace had no time to spare. Best thing to do, he decided, was to go back to Stockwell. Go back and shoot it out with Sheriff Petersen and his hired goons, and bust his dad out of jail. That's what he should have done instead of trying to find a way to prove Petersen and company were thieves. What did he care whether they were found out?

But it was like his mother had said: Bust Pop out of jail, and he'd be arrested again and maybe killed as a jail breaker.

No, not only did Ace have to get his dad out of jail,

163

he also had to get the goods on Sheriff Petersen and his deputies. Somehow it seemed important to show the whole damned county that their sheriff was a thief. Nobody would bother Pop then.

Think, damnit.

Finally, he tightened the cinch and mounted. Riding northwest, he continued trying to think of a way. When he came to Carrizo Creek, he turned the horse west. He remembered a low hill to the west of where the cattle were being worked. He'd be out of sight there and still be able to see the camp. Maybe he'd get lucky.

From where he lay on his belly, studying the camp a half mile ahead, Ace saw the crew branding the cattle that had been brought up the day before. Counting men, he knew that the three deputies were still there. They'd have the branding done well before dark. Would the deputies stay with the crew or go back to Stockwell? Ace figured they'd go back. They'd stay long enough to help brand their stolen cattle, but they wouldn't help trail the herd to Dodge. That wasn't their job. No, they'd go back to Stockwell. The question now was would they wait until next morning to leave or start home as soon as the branding was finished?

Either way, they'd be gone before Sheriff Reuben could gather some evidence and a posse. All Ace could do was watch and wait for a chance.

He went back to the horse, out of sight behind the hill, loosened the cinch, and hobbled its forefeet. "I don't know when I'll need you, pardner," he said to the animal, "but it won't be long."

His noon meal was a cold can of beans and a slice of bread. It tasted gosh-awful, but it was sustenance.

Watching, waiting, Ace tried again to formulate a plan. Nothing came to mind. If the three stayed the night, they'd have to pull their share of night guard, and maybe he could come up on one in the dark. It would take some luck, but maybe . . . Naw, the man wouldn't be taken without letting out a holler. That was asking for too much luck.

It was late afternoon when the last beef was branded down there and turned back to the herd. While Ace watched, the remuda was brought up. Three men caught fresh horses and changed saddles. Ace couldn't recognize them from that distance, but he hoped they were the deputies.

Sure enough, the three tied blanket rolls behind the cantles and mounted. Horseback, they talked a moment with George Alberts in his batwing chaps, then rode away, heading right for the hill that Ace was hiding behind.

"Well now," Ace said to the horse as he removed the hobbles, tightened the cinch, and mounted, "maybe things are going my way after all." But he had to stay out of their sight until he had his chance. To the north a mile was another low hill. He touched spurs to the blue roan and rode toward it at a gallop. "Don't worry, pardner, we ain't gonna run very far."

On the other side of the hill, he dismounted and crawled back to the crest on his hands and knees. Just in time. The deputies had started down the hill he'd been hiding behind. They'd see fresh horse manure. Would they wonder who'd been there? Would they be scared enough to go back to the cattle camp?

They stopped, studied the ground, looked around, turned Ace's way. Ace looked down, waited a half minute, then carefully raised his head enough to see them. They were going on, but glancing back now and then. Ace was glad he'd hidden the empty bean can.

Now it was a matter of following them, watching for a chance. Soon it would be dark and maybe they'd make

165

camp. Surely, they didn't plan on riding all night. He followed their tracks, constantly looking ahead to be sure he was out of their sight.

When it turned too dark to read the ground, he rode forward a few steps at a time, stopping and listening. They would camp soon. Last night was a moonless one. Can't be much of a moon tonight. They'd build a fire, making themselves easy to see. He'd be in the dark.

Soon, now.

Twenty-three

When he saw the dim glow of their camp fire, Ace Bailey stopped and dismounted. Men moved in the light of the fire. Afraid the horse's hoofbeats would be heard if he took it any closer, he dropped the reins. "Stay here," he whispered, though he knew the animal didn't understand. Now, he told himself, play Indian and see how close you can get. He walked carefully.

Coffee. They had coffee. Boy, did it smell good. Where were their horses? It was darker than the inside of a hip pocket. Now he was as close as he dared to be. One little sound would have them grabbing their guns.

They were hunkered down by the fire, sipping coffee, frying meat. The fire was nothing more than burning sagebrush, and it wouldn't burn long without being constantly fed. From where he was in the dark, Ace could have shot all three of them. But what would he gain by that? He had to get one man away from the others. How?

He got lucky.

One man stood and unsheathed a long skinning knife, saying something about cutting more sage. He walked away from the others. He walked in Ace's direction.

As long as the deputy was between him and the dim fire, Ace could see him clearly. But when he turned, looking for the largest of the sage bushes, he was out of

167

sight. Ace stood still, listening. He heard the hacking and cursing of a man cutting sage with a knife.

"Goddamn tough shit. Tougher'n a tree and burns like paper. Goddamn prairie."

Ace had to move, get the deputy between him and the fire again. Keep cussing, ol' buddy, he said under his breath. Keep cussing and hacking so you don't hear me. Moving one slow, careful step at a time, he got to where he could see the man. Now was the time to do it. Now while the man was busy. Still walking carefully, Ace came up behind him.

The deputy heard him, heard something, and he straightened, hand going for the six-gun on his right hip. Ace ran the last two steps. His left arm went around the deputy's throat; the .38 was in his right hand.

"Don't make a sound," Ace hissed through clenched teeth. But it was too late. The deputy let out a squawk like a chicken being grabbed by a coyote. He jumped, kicked, tried to turn around. "Don't move, you son of a bitch, or I'll shoot your spine in two." Still the deputy struggled, trying to turn and slash at Ace with the long-bladed knife. Ace kept a tight arm around his throat and dragged him backward to keep him off balance.

Now the two at the camp fire were standing, their guns drawn. They squinted into the dark, trying to find something to shoot at. The Colt .38 popped twice, rapidly. Both men were down.

"One more move and you'll die right here," Ace hissed. The deputy, seeing his two partners dead or dying, stopped struggling. "Drop that knife." The knife fell to the ground. "The gun, too, and be damned careful how you do it."

With the bore of the .38 against his right temple, the deputy slowly, carefully, lifted his six-gun from its holster and let it fall. "Who . . . who are you? Whatta you want?"

168

"I want you dead, you sorry son of a bitch. And that's exactly what you're gonna be if you don't do like I tell you."

"Whatta you want?"

"I'm gonna arrest you." Ace relaxed his hold on the deputy's throat and backed up a step.

"Arrest me? Are you a law officer?"

"Not hardly."

"You can't arrest me. I'm a deputy sheriff."

A snear crept into Ace's voice. "You're a thief."

"Whatta you gonna do?"

"Walk. Over there, where you're partners are. Be careful."

Back stiff, the deputy walked to the fire. Ace was two steps behind him, warning him, "One wrong move and you'll join your partners."

"Who . . . who are you?"

"You'll see."

At the camp, one of the downed deputies tried to rise but fell back, breathing raggedly. Keeping an eye on the standing one, Ace picked up the guns and threw them into the darkness. "On your belly," he ordered, pulling the handcuffs from his belt.

Once the man was down, hands shackled behind his back, Ace threw what remained of the cut sagebrush onto the fire. He stood in the firelight and asked, "Recognize me now?"

Lying on his belly, the deputy had to strain his neck muscles to raise his head. "Why you're . . . you're Ace Bailey."

"Now you know how close you came to being killed. I can cut you up in little pieces and cook you in this fire, or I can put a bullet in your sorry head."

"Don't . . . don't kill me."

"Where are your horses?"

"Over there."

"Over where? How far?"

"Over there where my head is pointing. Not more'n fifty feet. They're hobbled."

Looking around, Ace saw three saddles on the edge of the firelight. He picked up two bridles and went into the darkness. By getting the horses between him and the fire, and by sound and feel, Ace found them. He put bridles on two and turned the third one loose. Back at the camp, he wished he had more fuel for the fire, more light. What was burning wouldn't burn long. He had to work fast. He saddled the two horses and, leading one, went looking for the blue roan. It wasn't hard to find. Being a herd animal, the blue roan had sensed the other horses and had moved in their direction, dragging bridle reins. Working by feel, Ace pulled the saddle and bridle off. "You did your job, pardner," he said. "I appreciate it."

With little firelight to see by, Ace got the deputy mounted on one of the horses, hands still shackled behind his back. He mounted himself, hanging onto the reins of the deputy's horse. "You better hope this pony leads easy. And if you're thinking about jumping off and running in the dark, just remember there's nothing to hide behind here on the prairie and come daylight, I'll find you and kill you."

With a tight throat, the deputy asked, "Where . . . are we goin'?"

"To jail."

"Oh." Relief gave strength to the deputy's voice. "I'm an officer of the law. You can't lock me up in jail."

They were riding now, heading back toward Animas. "Keep talking," Ace said matter-of-factly, "and you'll talk me into killing you before we get there."

It would take the rest of the night to get back to Animas, which was fine with Ace. He wished he could deliver the deputy to the courthouse without being seen by

170

the townspeople, but he figured that would be impossible. With the North Star as a guide, he kept traveling in what he hoped was the right direction. The horses used their good night vision to keep from stumbling in the dark.

Now and then Ace looked back, but he couldn't see his prisoner. "Are you still there? Answer me."

"Yeah. You're making a mistake. You're the one that's gonna be arrested."

"Shut up."

When they crossed Carrizo Creek, Ace let the horses choose their way. They crossed at a spot that was easy for them but not so easy for the riders. Ace was almost dragged out of the saddle by a tree limb, and he heard the deputy grunt behind him. "Are you still on your horse?" he asked.

"Yeah, goddamnit, what're you tryin' to do? Kill me?"

"Shut up."

Hours later, a faint glow appeared on the eastern horizon. Another hour and Ace could see the wagon road to the south. Instead of traveling on the road, he stayed parallel with it. A mile from town he reined up.

"All right, get off your horse," he ordered.

"How the hell am I s'posed to get off with my hands behind my back?"

"Fall off."

On the ground, standing, Ace recognized his prisoner in the morning light. Yeah, he was one of the mean ones, one of the spectators at the beating Ace had taken in the Stockwell County jail. Sneering, he said, "You sorry son of a bitch, you ain't fit to live. Get off that horse before I drag you off."

The deputy got off awkwardly and fell onto his back. The horse snorted and sidestepped away from him.

"Stay down. Just stay where you are."

"What're we waitin' for?"

"For the courthouse to open."

"Hah. You're the one's gonna get locked up."

"Shut up."

At an estimated seven-thirty A.M., Ace got his prisoner and himself horseback, and headed toward the south side of Animas. "You don't say a damned word, understand? No matter how many questions folks ask, you don't say a damned word."

Questions were asked as the pair rode into town toward the courthouse. "Say, what's goin' on? Are you a marshal or a ranger, mister?"

"Yeah." Ace looked straight ahead.

"What's he done, mister?"

"He's a cattle thief."

A few men followed on foot, curiosity on their faces. At the courthouse, Ace said, "See if it's open, will you?"

A townsman in baggy wool pants and a floppy black hat tried the door. Locked. "Well," the man said, looking up the street, "here comes Old Tucker. He always opens 'er up."

Tucker turned out to be the man in the finger-length coat and white shirt who had unlocked the courthouse a day earlier. He stopped, eyes narrowed. "What's going on here?"

"We're waiting for Sheriff Reuben," Ace answered.

"He ain't here. Him and a couple of men rode out of here yesterday morning, and he said he probably wouldn't be back for two days, maybe longer."

"Well, this is one of the men he's looking for. I want him kept in the county jail 'til the sheriff gets back."

"Who are you? I don't re'clect seeing you before?"

"There's lots of law officers you haven't seen."

"Well . . ." Tucker thought it over a moment. "Well, bring him in."

"Listen, men," the deputy said, "I'm a deputy sheriff from New Mexico Territory. This man is Ace Bailey. He's

172

wanted all over the territory and half of Texas. He just murdered two of my partners."

Tucker's eyes and voice turned hard. "Is that right, mister?"

"Yep. I'm Ace Bailey, and this man is a thief. Sheriff Reuben knows all about him. He'd appreciate it if you would keep him locked up 'til he gets back."

"Is he really a deputy sheriff?"

"He is, but he's a cattle thief. Sheriff Reuben knows all about it."

"You're an outlaw yourself."

"I am, and I'm a killer. If I didn't think Jasper Reuben was an honest man, I'd have killed this son of a bitch instead of bringing him here. Now, are you gonna unlock this building?"

"Well, I want no traffic with a wanted man."

"Damn it, either unlock that door or you're gonna be responsible for this man's death." Turning to the small gathering, Ace said, "And I'd advise all of you to keep your guns in their holsters."

"Yessir, Mr. Bailey," said the man in the floppy hat. "There ain't a law officer in town, and we ain't gonna try to arrest you."

"Good. Now, Mr. Tucker, whatta you say?"

Reluctantly, Tucker said, "All right. As the county clerk and recorder, I'm in charge of this building. I'll lock him up until Sheriff Reuben returns."

Dismounted, Ace helped his prisoner off his horse and guided him inside the building behind the county officer. Upstairs, in a jail cell, Ace ordered the deputy to sit on the floor, then pulled his boots off. The deputy whined, "You're making a mistake, Mr. Tucker. When the sheriff gets back, you'll find out."

Ignoring him, Ace said "I ain't got a key to these handcuffs." The county clerk and recorder went through the sheriff's desk until he found a key. Ace unlocked the

173

shackles, stepped outside the cell, and locked the door.

"You can feed him if you want to, but I'd advise you not to touch him. Be careful. If you think I'm a killer . . . he's a hell of a lot more dangerous than I am."

"Where are you going?"

A wry grin turned up the corners of Ace's mouth. "In a day or two this town is gonna be lousy with lawmen. I intend to be far away." With that, he turned on his heels and went down the stairs.

Outside, a dozen men had gathered, but no one made a threatening move. They only stared. Acc stepped into the saddle of one of the two horses, a dun with high withers and a long neck and back. "Kindly take this other horse to the livery barn, will you?"

"Yeah," a man said.

"Thanks. *Adios,* gents."

Twenty-four

Ace Bailey rode west at a slow trot, glancing behind him now and then to be sure he wasn't being followed. He had a terrible urgency to get home, but he knew the horse could travel only so fast. He also needed sleep and grub. He crossed Carrizo Creek far to the west, far enough that nobody from the Mill Iron would see him, and there he stopped, unsaddled and hobbled the horse. He left the bridle on, believing the animal wouldn't go far hobbled and dragging bridle reins. The horse was more interested in cropping the grass and weeds along the creek than in leaving. Bailey lay on his back in the weeds, put his hat over his face to keep the flies off, and slept.

At noon he resaddled and continued his journey, angling northwest. His eyes were constantly scanning the country around him. Sheriff Reuben and his deputies would be returning about now, perhaps with a posse of cattlemen. Ace didn't want to be seen.

His stomach growled and grumbled, and he remembered a gunnysack containing some bread and canned food he'd left ahead near the two dead men. About an hour before sundown he found them. The dead deputies had attracted a small cloud of flies and so had their grub. But the gunnysack was drawing no flies and was where Ace had left it. He picked up the sack and rode

175

on until dusk, out of the sight and smell of the dead men.

In a fold between two low hills, he stopped and let the horse graze while he ate a can of beans and half a loaf of bread. Then, just before dark, he mounted and rode on.

"We ought to get home about daylight," he said to the horse.

It was a tired man and horse that approached the Bailey farm shortly after first light. As before, Ace rode around the buildings, studying everything. He rode up to the barn and peered between cracks in the grey, warped boards without getting off his horse. In spite of the near darkness inside the barn, he could see the two large shapes of the Baileys' harness team, but nothing more.

Mrs. Bailey came outside, carrying a pail, ready to milk the one milk cow. When Ace rode around the corner of the barn, she dropped the bucket and turned to run back inside.

"Mom," Ace yelled, "it's me."

She stopped, recognizing her son. A weak smile divided her weathered, work-worn face. "Alvin. Thank God you're back."

"Anybody else around?"

"There's nobody now. Put your horse in the barn and come in."

Inside, Ace asked, "How's Pop? When did you see him last?"

The lines in his mother's face had deepened, and she spoke with anxiety. "He's not well, Alvin. I don't think he'll live much longer in jail. What happened to your neck? Did you get shot?"

Fingering the wound, he said, "It's scabbing over. I'm going to get Pop out."

176

"How, Alvin?"

"Sheriff Petersen ain't got as many deputies now as he did the last time I was here."

Mrs. Bailey had a fire going in the cookstove, and she fried boar belly and hot cakes. Coffee was brewing. Talking around a mouthful of food, Ace said, "There's gonna be a rider from Animas, Texas in a few days carrying a message to Garrison at the store. The message will prove Sheriff Petersen and his toughs are cattle thieves."

Sitting opposite him at the table, Mrs. Bailey asked, "Will they let the reverend out of jail then?"

"I'm not waiting."

"Poor Mr. Bailey."

"Mom, do you think Pop can stand one more day in jail?"

A long sigh came out of his mother. "I reckon. Poor Mr. Bailey. He's always abided by the Good Book and the law, now look how the law has treated him."

"The law's like that." Ace chewed thoughtfully. "But in the long run, I think it'll work." He chewed and swallowed. "Some of the time, anyway."

"You look tired, Alvin."

"Yeah, I could use some rest, but mainly I want that horse to rest a day. I'll have to do some more riding."

"You're gonna leave again, then?"

"I'll have to."

His mother's face had a sad, long look. "Are you gonna be runnin' and hidin' the rest of your life, Alvin?"

"I'm gonna change my ways, Mom. As soon as I get Pop out of jail, I'm gonna head west, get out of the territory, and maybe even quit carrying a gun."

"Nothin' would make me and your dad happier than havin' you change your ways and quit runnin'. Now that Jim's dead, you're the only son we've got."

He shaved with his dad's straight razor, then took a bath in a stock tank while his mother washed his clothes.

177

Brother Jim's clothes were a little big in the waist, but they kept him covered until his own clothes dried. The dun horse was fed all the maize it wanted and was watered twice that day. At night, Ace carried some blankets out by the barn where he slept, not wanting to be trapped inside the house. In the morning he ate a big breakfast, then he was ready.

"Wish me luck, Mom."

"I'll pray for you, Alvin."

"That too." He kissed his mother good-bye, mounted the dun horse, and rode up the road to Stockwell.

Why did he have the feeling he would never see his mother again? He wasn't worried about what Sheriff Petersen would do. That didn't worry him at all. But somehow, in the back of his mind, he had the feeling he would never again see the Bailey farm or his mother.

Well rested and well fed, he wanted to get this chore over. There would never be a better time.

He'd thought about it. There was no use trying to be tricky, setting a trap or anything. No use going to see Garrison at the mercantile. There was only one way to do it. With luck, it would be over before midmorning.

Stockwell was quiet. Ace rode down the main street at a walk. His eyes took in everything. A woman came out of the mercantile, carrying a covered basket. Her long dress dragged on the boardwalk. A buggy, pulled by one horse, was ahead of him. The saloon was open but quiet. There were no horses tied in front of it, nor in front of the Stockwell County sheriff's office and jail. He rode past two men who were standing on the boardwalk by the harness shop, talking. One glanced up, did a double take, and stared. He whispered something to the other man, who also stared.

Ace reined up in front of the sheriff's office and dismounted, moving like a man going on about his business. But that tingling was there—in his knees, stomach, and hands. He paused only a second, then opened the door to the sheriff's office and stepped inside.

Disappointment. Sheriff Petersen wasn't there. There was only one deputy, a husky man in rider's boots who was sitting tilted back in a wooden chair at the desk. He looked up, annoyed at being disturbed by a citizen this early in the morning. Then his eyes bugged out and his hand went for the six-gun on his hip.

"Morning," Ace said. The Colt .38 jumped into his hand, and an exploding cartridge filled the room with noise and gunsmoke.

The dead deputy folded at the waist, then pitched forward onto the floor. The back of his head had opened up like an overripe melon.

Still moving like a man going on about his business, Ace went through the desk until he found the jail key. He opened the connecting door and saw his dad standing near the bunk. A mixture of puzzlement, surprise, and gladness spread over the Reverend Bailey's face.

"Alvin? What . . . what happened, Alvin?" He was thin. His cheekbones were barely covered with flesh and pasty white skin. His eyes were hollow and sunken.

At the sight of his father, the tingling turned to anger. Explosive anger. But he swallowed a lump in his throat and kept his voice calm. "I came to get you out, Pop. You can go home now. Let Mom take care of you." He unlocked the cell door and swung it open. "Wait just a minute. This ain't quite over. Won't be long." He turned on his heels and went outside.

The single gunshot had attracted attention. Two men and a woman came out of the mercantile down the street, and they stared in his direction. Another man across the street was standing as if petrified. The two in front of the blacksmith shop were both staring with open mouths. The horse-drawn buggy was hitched in front of the hardware store next door. Another man took off, running around the corner of the mercantile.

Ace stood in the open doorway, protected from three sides. He leaned his left shoulder against the doorjamb. The .38 was in its holster. He waited.

Minutes went by. Nobody moved. Another minute. Ace was beginning to feel nervous. Come on, you sonofabitch, his mind said. He forced himself to be calm, to concentrate on the gun on his hip. Which way would the sheriff come from? Would he be alone or would he have some deputies with him? He waited.

And then he came. From around the corner of the mercantile, carrying a double-barreled shotgun, he came. It was him, all right. The high cheekbones, the long downturned moustache, the narrow, cruel eyes. He was coming on the run—until he saw Ace standing in the doorway.

He stopped suddenly, threw the shotgun to his shoulder, and fired. The distance was about a hundred yards, easy range for the gun. But the sheriff had fired too hastily. Buckshot peppered the ground in front of his office. Petersen cocked the hammer behind the second barrel, ready to fire again.

Two rapid shots came from Ace Bailey, standing in the doorway. One slug hit Petersen in the right shoulder and the other tore into his throat. He spun and fell. His life's blood spurted out of the jugular vein into the dirt.

Stockwell was quiet again. Nobody moved, only stared, eyes going from the dying sheriff to Ace Bailey.

Finally, Ace holstered the .38, and yelled, "Garrison. Mr. Garrison. Come over here."

The plump, red-faced grocer, his baggy wool pants held up with suspenders, took a step forward and stopped. "What . . . who . . . whatta you want, Bailey?"

Still standing in the doorway, protected from three sides, Ace yelled, "Come over here. I'm through shooting. I need to talk to you."

180

Garrison took two more steps, then stopped again. Another man stepped up beside him, a tall, thin man in bib overalls. "Alvin," he hollered, "do you remember me? I've knowed the reverend for a long time, and I knowed you when you was a pup."

Ace recognized him then, a neighbor he hadn't seen in at least six years. "I recognize you, Mr. Bunche. Come over here, both of you. I wouldn't shoot a neighbor."

They approached, Garrison warily, Bunche boldly. Ace said, "Mr. Garrison, a rider is coming from Animas, Texas in a few days with proof that Sheriff Petersen and his deputies were cattle thieves. He might bring some warrants and some help with him. I don't know. What I want you to do right now is take my dad home. He's sick and he needs help. You help him, hear?"

Garrison only nodded. Bunche said, "I'll do 'er, Alvin. That's my rig over there." He nodded at the horse and buggy. "I'll take him home for you."

"Thanks, Mr. Bunche. I remember you as a good neighbor." To Garrison, he said, "I don't want nobody bothering my folks. They've broke no laws and nobody bothers them again, ever. I won't be so far away that I can't come back."

"Y—yes . . . uh . . . Alvin," the grocer stammered.

With that, Ace went to the dun horse, unwrapped the reins from the hitchrail, and swung into the saddle. Looking down at Garrison, he said, "Next time you elect a sheriff, pick an honest man."

He rode away at a trot, heading west. His back was a good target. Townspeople watched him, but no one moved until he was almost out of sight.

Twenty-five

It was going to be a good day for the Bailey family. Reverend Bailey was out of jail and at home with Mrs. Bailey, it was going to rain—something the Bailey farm needed badly—and Ace was in no immediate danger.

He stayed on the wagon road where traveling was easy, and he kept the dun horse going at a slow, steady trot. When thunder rolled over the country, he smiled. Getting wet was nothing new to him. The rain, when it came, was a slow drizzle, the kind that soaked the ground and made the grass and crops grow.

By mid afternoon he was in sight of Mount Capulin and south of the range of mountains. He didn't stop. He had nothing to eat, anyway. Rain water was dripping off his hat brim. His shirt was stuck to his back. The drizzle was not a warm one, and he shivered at times. He knew lawmen would soon be after him again, and he couldn't stay long in one place. But for the time being, he was riding in the daylight.

Enough daylight was left for him to see only one horse in Uncle Amos's corral. It was the bay gelding that Marybelle Stewart had given him. He figured Uncle Amos was using the horse to wrangle in his other horses when he needed them.

"Uncle Amos," he yelled.

Amos Bailey opened the door to his one-room cabin and peered into the near darkness.

"It's me, Alvin."

"Alvin. Come in this house, Alvin. Put your horse in the pen and feed him some hay and come in here."

With his hands wrapped around a hot cup of coffee and his clothes drying in the warmth of the room, Ace felt better than he'd felt in a long time. No, his uncle had told him, nobody had been around asking questions lately. But how was the reverend?

Ace told him all about it. Uncle Amos was both sad and glad. "They say ever'body accused of a crime is s'posed to get a trial," he said, "but a man can die in jail waitin'. I'm sure glad you busted him out, and I'm glad that damned sheriff ain't gonna be able to arrest him again. But they'll be after you as hard as ever, Alvin. You're gettin' to be the most famous outlaw in the territory. I even read about you in the newspaper. Here." Uncle Amos went to a wooden box on the far side of the room, opened its hinged top, and took out a copy of the *Raton Range*. "I kept this for you. Here, read about yourself."

The story filled the bottom quarter of page one. It read:

"Ace Bailey, the killer wanted by law officers all over New Mexico Territory, added to his fame recently by again exercising his skill with a six-shooter. This time, however, his victim was not a human being, but a bear. Cowboys who drove a herd of cattle from the heart of the Sangre de Cristos to the south end of Colfax County brought the bear's hide to town and sold it for an undisclosed sum of money to William Eastman, owner of the Railroad Emporium. The cowboys, working for the Cross Seven Ranch, said the animal was shot by Ace Bailey.

"Now nailed to a wall in the saloon, the hide measures over six feet from one end to the other without the head. It is the hide of a silvertip male, and one of the largest ever seen in the Territory.

183

"Cowboys said Mr. Bailey showed up in their camp about ten days ago, and as the crew was shorthanded, he was given a job helping move a large herd of cattle out of the mountains. They said he gave his name as Alvin Bailey, believed to be his real name, and was a quiet, unassuming young man of good nature. When they drove the herd past the spot where the bear had been killed a few days earlier, Mr. Bailey told the cowboys about it. They said the bear had been shot in the head six times, something that only an expert pistol marksman could do. Not until then did the cowboys suspect that Alvin Bailey and the infamous Ace Bailey were one and the same.

"According to two of the Cross Seven cowboys, Ace Bailey drew his wages after the herd reached the flatlands, and he was last seen riding south. They said he told them he was going to Albuquerque. Law officers in Albuquerque have been alerted by telegraph to be on the lookout for him. Although he was described by the cowboys as showing no belligerent tendencies, he is known to be extremely dangerous.

"Meanwhile, the bear's hide is attracting a large number of curiosity seekers, and Mr. Eastman said his saloon business has grown considerably."

Ace had to grin a lopsided grin when he finished reading. "Well, whatta you know."

"Did they exaggerate, Alvin?"

"No," Ace grinned. "No, it's true."

Uncle Amos grinned with him. "They can write all kinds of tall tales about you without stretchin' the truth."

"This is nothing. Wait 'til the newspapers find out about what happened in Stockwell this morning. And in Animas, Texas."

Shaking his head negatively but grinning at the same time, Uncle Amos allowed, "Hell, one of these days I'm gonna be famous just for being a kin of yours. Hell, when I get old, I'll be able to stand up at a bar and drink all night just for talkin' about you."

At that, Ace had to laugh. "Don't go getting the swells, Uncle Amos."

They stuffed themselves with elk steaks, boiled potatoes, carrots, and Amos Bailey's baking soda biscuits. The older man rolled a cigarette, tilted his chair on its hind legs, and asked, "Where're you goin' next, Alvin?"

"Well . . ." Ace turned his chair sideways, stretched his legs, and put his hands behind his head. "I've got an idea. I'll prob'ly be wasting my time, but there's something I just have to see about."

They were silent a moment. The older man smoked. Then, exasperated, he said, "Well hell, Alvin, you gonna tell this old man about it?"

Shaking his head, Ace said, "If I make a fool of myself, I won't want anybody to know." He chuckled, "Might muddy my reputation. And if I'm right, you'll hear everything."

The older man knew it was useless to pry, so he changed the subject. "When're you leavin'?"

"In the morning. I think I can ride in the daylight for a while."

"Yeah." Amos Bailey turned serious. "For a day or two. Then they'll be after you. If I was you, I'd stay out of the towns where you might be recognized. What you ought to do is get plumb out of the country. Head west. I hear Arizoney's a good country."

"I've been thinking about that. I'd sure like to see Mindy. 'Specially after her baby is born. But I'd prob'ly better stay away for a while. I don't know what kind of law dogs they've got over at Cimarron."

"I don't know nothin' about 'em." Uncle Amos shook his head sadly. "Too bad you can't visit your own sister."

"I will one of these days."

He left next morning, angling southwest, riding the dun horse with a blanket roll and a sack of grub tied behind the cantle. The rain had turned the hills green overnight, and the air smelled fresh and clean. Small red flowers decorated the cane cactus, and the yucca bells were in full bloom. Ace Bailey took his time, enjoying the morning. He stayed south of Raton, and when he came to the cattle trail he had once followed east, he stopped. While the horse grazed, he ate cold biscuits and bacon, and drank out of a trickle of a stream that the rain had created. Then he cinched up and traveled on to the banks of the Vermejo River.

He wasn't far from Cimarron now, and his thoughts went again to his sister. She would be a mother soon. He'd be an uncle. What would the child be told about his—or her—Uncle Alvin? Would he—or she—grow up thinking of Uncle Alvin as the man who'd gotten rid of a crooked sheriff at Stockwell, or as a dangerous outlaw?

Lord, he wished he could be a regular uncle.

His supper was more bacon, fried that morning, and bread and beans warmed over a small fire. He lay in his blankets, listening to the gentle slapping of the river water on the rocks and banks, listening to his horse graze.

By mid morning the next day he was working his way down into Van Bremmer Canyon, still going back over the cattle trail. In places the canyon cliffs were a variety of colors due to the assortment of minerals exposed by centuries of wind and rain. Ace stayed north of Wheeler Peak, and by dark he was on the other side of Bobcat Pass in the Sangre de Cristos.

Traveling was up and down hills the next day, but it was easy compared to driving a herd of cattle over the hills. He passed the spot where he'd killed the bear, and then he had one more range of hills to climb to get to his destination.

Rolled up in his blankets that night, he wondered if he was making the trip for nothing. It was a fool's idea. He ought to be heading for Phoenix or going down to El Paso, where he could sleep in a soft bed, eat female-cooked meals, and yes, sleep with a woman.

The early morning sun was at his back, casting long shadows ahead of him as he rode up the last ridge. It was a hard climb, and he promised the horse it would graze on good grass and rest for at least a day before it had to climb more mountains. He rode down from the ridge, across a small creek, around a pile of house-sized boulders, through a stand of tall pine and spruce, and he was there.

The cabin, what remained of it, was exactly as he'd remembered it. The hanging tree stood over the grave across the creek from the cabin. The remains of a horse corral were there. So were the ashes from his own camp fire. Riding around the place, he saw no sign of anyone having been there. He had the valley to himself.

"Well, pardner," he said, reaching down and scratching the horse's neck, "here's where I make a pile of money.

"Or make a fool of myself."

Twenty-six

Thirty-two thousand dollars in double eagles, the woman had said. That was a lot of coins to hide, but there was a lot of territory to hide it in. Where to look?

Ace Bailey offsaddled and hobbled the dun horse, stood in front of the cabin, and ran it through his mind. "Let's see," he mused aloud. "Here's the way it was: A bunch of marauding Indians, probably Apaches who'd quit one of the reservations, attacked and killed four train robbers. They took the robbers' guns, their surviving horses, and their loot.

"Now then, all that gold was worthless to Indians. They couldn't just ride into a town and buy what they wanted. They couldn't spend any of it—unless they knew of a white man who would do their buying for them.

"'Tate,' the man's name was. Tate had a reputation for trading with Indians. He'd buy guns or whatever the Indians wanted and sell it to them for a big profit. He'd steal horses and sell them to the Indians. The Indians didn't kill Tate because they needed him. How much did they trust him? The whites around here sure didn't trust him. He was hung for stealing horses from the Cross Seven. That grave over there is where Tate's body is buried. Tate lived in this cabin.

"Did the Indians leave the gold with Tate? Nobody on the Cross Seven mentioned any gold. If Tate had it, he'd hidden it. It was still here.

"All right, start looking."

188

He stepped through the door and took in the room. It was the way he remembered it — the collapsed roof, the sections of stovepipe, the rotted and broken floorboards, the pack rat's nest, the spilled flour and sugar. Was there a shovel? There had to be a shovel.

Outside, he walked across what remained of the pole corral, looked inside the lean-to shed. Yeah, it took a shovel to dig those post holes. Old Tate prob'ly used the shovel to bury the gold. In fact, Adam Potter and the Cross Seven men had used a shovel to dig Tate's grave. Find the shovel.

It was easy to find. The executioners had buried Tate and had thrown the shovel aside. It was lying in the tall grass along the creek. The long handle had been made of pressure-treated wood and was badly weathered but still in one piece. Now where to dig?

Carrying the shovel, Bailey walked around, head down, trying to guess. There wasn't a clue. In six years the grass and weeds had grown over everything. How long had it taken the grass to grow over freshly dug dirt? A year at least. Old Tate wouldn't leave fresh dirt where it could be seen. Where would it not be seen? Nowhere.

But Tate had horses. Horses trampled the dirt.

When the thought struck Bailey, he walked with quick steps to the corral. Sure. If Tate had buried something and didn't want to arouse anybody's suspicion, he'd have buried it in the corral where horses' hooves would have covered any trace of digging. But at the corral, he shook his head sadly. The ground had been trampled so hard that only a few weeds grew there. He couldn't dig up the whole damned corral.

"Aw, damnit," he said aloud, "I've got as much chance of finding that gold as a whore has of finding the pearly gates."

He stood with his head down, trying to think. Now then, if Old Tate had buried the loot in this corral, he alone would know exactly where. He'd measured the distance from some point. What point? One of the corners? Which corner, and how far? Did he have it memorized or had he written it down?

If he'd put it in writing on a piece of paper, where would the paper be?

Bailey dropped the shovel and went back to the cabin. A few ragged pieces of clothing hung from nails on what remained of the walls. He went through the pockets of a pair of dirty overalls and found nothing but a dried piece of plug tobacco. When he searched the pockets of a dirty shirt, the rotten cloth tore in his hands. More clothing could be under the collapsed wall.

Straining the muscles in his legs and back, working up a sweat, Bailey managed to lift one end of the collapsed wall and look under it. Sure enough, there was an old mackinaw and a gunnysack. He dragged the piece of a wooden chair over and used it to prop up the wall, then he crawled. If the chair broke, the wall would fall on him and he could be hurt. This was a bad place to be hurt. Moving carefully, breathing with shallow breaths, he crawled under the wall and got the sack and mackinaw in his hands. On his belly, he backed out and heaved a sigh of relief when he was able to stand.

"Aw, damnit."

The gunnysack contained two cans of something and a sack of moldy dried fruit. The cans were so old that the labels were unreadable. A pair of leather gloves had been stuffed into the pockets of the mackinaw. The leather was dried and twisted. There was nothing more.

Disheartened, Bailey went outside and saw that his horse was happily cropping the mountain grass. He unrolled his blankets and ate a meal of canned beef and bread.

This was hopeless. Men had spent years looking for hidden gold. Damned if he'd do that. Hell, he wasn't even sure there was gold hidden here. How long should he look?

Well, he decided, he'd give it a day. No more. If he hadn't found anything by this time tomorrow, he'd leave. Forget it. Head south. See how far he could go before he had to spend the last of his Cross Seven wages on grub. Going into a store was taking a chance on being recognized, but he had to eat. Maybe he could buy something from a Mexican farmer.

Back to the corral. If he himself was going to bury anything here, he'd pick a spot that he could easily remember. That meant in the middle. Bailey started digging.

Damned hard ground. He jumped on the shovel, hacked at the ground with it, pried rocks out with the tip of it, picked rocks out with his hands. After an hour and a half, he had found nothing but rocks. And the shovel handle broke.

That, by God, ended that.

Digging was useless, anyway. Old Tate could have paced off a distance from any tree — ten paces, twenty, due north or due east or . . .

What was the use?

He went back inside the cabin and ran his fingers through the spilled sugar and flour, hoping to find a note hidden in it. He studied the walls, what remained of them. Directions could have been written on something besides paper. He went out to the lean-to and examined the walls, looking for a penciled message.

Well hell, he decided finally, the secret of hidden gold — if there was any gold — was buried with Tate. Unless . . .

There was another place to look.

He'd heard of women, afraid of robbers, hiding money under floorboards. That was a possibility. Inside again, he started pulling up rotten, broken boards. He could pull up every board in the place before dark if he had to. Working, sweating, he pulled, pried, and piled the broken pieces outside. Rusty nails creaked.

He'd pulled up over half the floor when he stopped a moment to straighten his back and rest. It occurred to him that if Tate had buried something under the floor, he'd have cut a hole in the floorboards. Or, more than likely, he'd buried it where two ends met. Yeah, he could have pried up the ends and then nailed them back. Well, now. The ends met in the middle. Bailey had already pulled up half the floor. Let's see now.

No, there was nothing in the middle that looked like a hiding place.

Bailey went back to the corral and picked up the shovel with a broken handle, brought it back inside, and scraped the ground with it. Nothing. He pulled up more boards and scraped the ground under them.

Aw, what was the use?

It was quiet in the cabin while Bailey rested and stretched his back. The big grey pack rat came from somewhere and headed for its nest. It stopped, sat on its hind end, stared at the wreckage, and scampered back through a crack in the wall.

"I made a mess of the place, didn't I?" Ace said. "I hate to say this, but about the only spot left is under your nest."

The nest was made of grass, twigs, bits of cloth, and splinters of wood. Carefully, Bailey scooped it up with both hands, trying not to tear it apart. Under it, the floorboards were solid. Ace sat it down and turned to study the floorboards. Then his head swiveled back to the nest.

It was made of grass, twigs, bits of cloth, splinters—and something metallic.

The first thought that went through Bailey's mind was that it was a nail. Pack rats liked to pick up a nail or

192

anything shiny and carry it around until they found something more interesting. As a kid, he'd often had to sift through the grain before feeding the horses. Pack rats had carried nails or anything else they found until they came to the grain, and then they traded. That's why they were sometimes called trade rats.

But out of curiosity, Ace used his fingers to dig the piece of metal out of the nest.

He sucked in his breath.

It was round. It was flat. It was a coin.

For a long moment he couldn't believe it. The coin was a dirty grey color and could have been made of lead for all Ace knew. He rubbed it on his pants leg. He spat on it and rubbed it again. The grey was coming off. It was gold.

Jumping to his feet, he yelled, "Hallclujah. It's gold. I found it."

But no, he hadn't found it. The rat had found it.

He let his breath out slowly. Could it be that Old Tate had had one or two gold coins and the rat had found one of them? Yeah, that could be. But it was also possible the rat had found thirty-two thousand dollars worth of gold coins.

All right, now, think.

The coins had to be somewhere near. They had to be hidden where only a rat would find them. Under the floor. Sure as hell.

"Hate to wreck your home, feller," Ace said, using the shovel tip to pry up boards under where the nest had been. "You can build a new home in a few days." Grunting, straining, he added, "But it ain't every day a man finds a fortune."

When he pulled up the last section of wood he saw the rotten burlap. It was buried with only a small piece showing. Hastily, he grabbed the shovel and, working furiously, scratched and scraped. He tore the bag open.

193

Then he was running his fingers through hundreds of gold coins.

"Whoa," he said, rocking back on his heels. "It ain't real. It can't be real. It is real. There ain't this much money in the whole world. Yes, there is. It's right here. Whoa!"

Walking like a man in a daze, he went outside and sat on the ground. Not one chance in a hundred of finding that gold, but he'd found it. He threw his head back and let out a howl like a lobo wolf. He'd found it. Hallelujah.

The dun horse looked at him as if wondering what that human animal was up to now.

Still shaking his head and grinning, Ace got to his feet. All right, now, how to get it to town? To town? Hell, he'd have to carry it a long ways before he could spend it. Well, maybe he could spend a little of it.

But he had to have a way to carry it.

After worrying about it a while, he went back inside and put a few of the coins in his pockets. Then he carefully replaced the pieces of floorboards over the open burlap bag, carefully picked up the rat's nest with both hands, and put it back where he'd found it.

Outside, he went to the horse, took the hobbles off, and led the animal to the creek. "Take a good drink, pardner. Eat. Rest. Tomorrow we'll be traveling again.

"I think we'll take a little trip down to Santa Fe."

Twenty-seven

By sunup he was on his way, going almost straight south over rocky hills, around piles of boulders, through tall timber, following burro trails and no trails. He spent the night on the banks of the Rio Chiquito, where he ate the last of his grub. At noon the next day he cut over to the Rio Grande and followed a wagon road to the ramshackle settlement of Espanola, where he stopped long enough to buy two cans of sardines and a loaf of bread. Across the river, out of sight of the road, he ate, let the horse rest, then went on. By dusk he was at the north end of Santa Fe.

The smart thing to do, he decided, was to ride right up to The Red Rose Saloon, tie his horse to a hitchrail, and walk in. Santa Fe was the territorial capitol, the crossroads to everywhere, the biggest trading center in the Southwest. Strangers, ragged travelers, were common. He might be lucky enough to go unrecognized. For a short time.

On the other hand, suppose he was recognized and had to shoot it out and run for it. He'd need a well-fed and rested horse.

On the outskirts of town he saw a Mexican pitching hay to two horses in a juniper corral. He rode up. "Evening, *senor*," he said pleasantly.

The Mexican, an old man with thick grey hair and a brown wrinkled face, nodded and smiled a broken-toothed smile.

"Sabe usted Inglés?"

"Poquito. Poco."

"I need feed and rest for this horse. I'll pay you a dollar to feed him and keep him here tonight."

The old man thought it over and nodded his head. *"Un dollar?"*

Digging into his pants pocket, Ace produced a silver dollar. "This one."

"Si." The old man's head nodded more vigorously.

Dismounting, Ace pulled off the saddle, led the horse to a wooden water trough, and let it drink its fill. Then he led it inside the corral and gently took the pitchfork from the old man's hands. "I'll feed him myself." That done, he handed over the dollar. "Feed him again early in the morning, and I'll give you another dollar."

With a wide grin, the Mexican, said, *"Si, senor.* I will do that, you betcha. *Si."*

Ace left the saddle, blanket roll, everything he owned, on the ground beside the corral and walked. It wasn't far to a fine big Catholic mission, and from there only a short walk to the plaza. Standing on a plank sidewalk under a flat roof held up by pine poles, he saw The Red Rose. By now it was dark, but the plaza was lighted with a dozen lamps, and people of three races were strolling casually through it. There were men in business suits with brocaded vests and pointed shoes; there were men in baggy overalls and brogan shoes; there were Mexicans in tight leggings, gaily decorated vests, and huge hats with embroidered brims. And there were Indians with round expressionless faces, wrapped in blankets with long hair hanging down their backs like horses' tails.

The smell of cooking food was strong in the plaza, and Bailey's stomach grumbled. But he had an errand, a message to deliver, and he walked rapidly across the plaza to The Red Rose.

Everything a man could want was inside: a long polished bar of hand-carved oak, a long mirror with gilted trim, whiskey bottles of every size and shape, a dance floor, card tables, music, women. Paradise. This was the way to live. A man with Ace Bailey's gambling skills could spend the rest of his life in here without doing a lick of work, without hoeing and grubbing, without sleeping on rocks, without eating jerked meat.

No one paid him any attention when he stepped up to the bar and ordered whiskey, good Kentucky bourbon. The bartender frowned at the gold coin, bounced it on the palm of his hand, rubbed it with his thumb, then shrugged. The only person in the huge room who gave Bailey a second look was himself—when he saw his reflection in the big mirror behind the bar.

He needed a shave, a haircut, a bath, and clean clothes. He looked wilder than any Indian—like a man who'd been too long away from civilization.

Well, he toasted himself in the mirror, you won't look this way much longer. You've got enough money to buy anything you want.

"Where'd ya come from, mister?"

Ace had made a mistake. The man standing next to him was giving him a second look. He was a working man, but he was clean, freshly shaven, and he smelled of bay rum.

"Oh . . . uh . . . west."

"Been trappin'? Huntin'?"

"Yeah, hunting."

"Was that a double eagle?"

"Yeah."

"That's the only kind of money a feller can trust. This U.S. gover'ment paper might turn out to be worthless."

The man had a lean face and white skin around his ears where—until recently—his head had been covered with hair. He looked and smelled as if he'd just come from a barber shop. But Bailey wasn't interested in a conversation with him, and his eyes scanned the room. There were a lot of people, a lot of women. He saw her.

Marybelle Stewart wore a red dress that was so low in front her breasts almost spilled out. And it was high enough at the bottom to show trim ankles and calves. Her long chestnut hair had been combed and brushed until it shone under the etched glass lamps. A red rose was pinned at the bottom of the deep V in her dress, and another decorated the left side of her hair. She was smiling a gleaming smile, circulating, saying pleasant things to the men.

Somehow she felt him staring at her and their eyes met.

For a second—only a second—her smile slipped and her eyes widened. Immediately, the smile returned, and she resumed saying pleasant things. But she was working her way over to Ace, not hurrying, spending a few seconds smiling at a well-dressed gent with slicked-back hair. Ace sipped his whiskey and waited.

"Well, hello, stranger," she said at his elbow. "You look like a man who's been traveling."

He shot her a glance and said out of the corner of his mouth, "I need to talk to you."

"Where are you from?" The gleaming smile was turned his way. "Did you come in with a wagon train?" She edged in between the man and Ace.

Before saying any more, Ace held out one of the gold coins. Her smile slipped again, and a "Huh?" came from her throat.

"Goddamn, you're beautiful." He was smiling, too.

"Where . . . uh . . . what? . . ."

"Keep smiling. Two day's ride. We have to leave early in the morning. You'll need a good horse, two pairs of big saddlebags, enough chuck for four days, and if you can get hold of a rifle, bring that, too."

"That will take time. I can't do a thing tonight."

"All right, I'll get the saddlebags and the chuck."

"Where will we meet?"

"There's a Mexican's 'dobe shack on the north end, just east of where the road comes down from Espanola. He's got a stick corral and three horses. One of the horses, a dun gelding, is mine. Be there by sunup. Keep smiling."

She was smiling. Around the smile, in a low voice, she said, "I'll be there."

"Goddamn, you're beautiful." He tossed down the rest of his whiskey and left.

Santa Fe's biggest industry was government and its second biggest was trading. Bailey had no trouble finding a store open late, which sold everything he wanted, including two U.S. Army saddlebags, the kind that hung from the pommel. Checking into a hotel was risky, but so far no one had given him a second glance. He picked a two-story wooden hotel with no bathing facilities and a toilet out back. His room was on the second floor, with a window over a dark alley. If he had to, he could jump out the window and maybe disappear in the dark.

He didn't get under the heavy quilt on the bed but lay on top, taking off only his boots. Under his breath, he said, "I hope there's no livestock in this bed, the kind with legs on both sides." He slept.

The dun horse was munching hay when Ace walked back to the Mexican's corral. He handed over a silver dollar, which was change from the twenty-dollar gold piece he'd handed the bartender, and saddled the horse. The "wither bags" he'd bought were made to fit over the pommel of an army saddle, so he cut holes in the middle leathers to get them to fit over a saddle horn. While the horse resumed eating, he waited.

Marybelle Stewart showed up on horseback and ready for travel, wearing bib overalls, a man's shirt, and a wide-brimmed hat with her hair tucked under it. In spite of that, she was an attractive woman. A lever-action rifle was in a boot under her right leg. The old Mexican stood back and watched them with curiosity.

"*Gracias*," Ace said as they rode past the old man, headed for the cedar hills. At Espanola, they quit the wagon road and took to the mountains, following the same route Ace had come over the day before. When they stopped at noon and ate a meal of bread and canned beef, he had to tell her how he'd found the gold.

"It was luck," he concluded. "Pure luck."

"Luck, and adding two and two."

"The chances of finding it were so small, if I'd had anything better to do, I prob'ly wouldn't even have looked."

"Is there any chance of someone else coming along and finding it before we can get back there?"

"Naw. Not likely. Nobody'd been there for years."

"I'll feel safer when we get it in our saddlebags."

"Yeah." Ace stood, walked back a ways, then returned. She said, "I see you looking behind us all the time. Are you afraid we might be followed?"

"There's always that chance, I reckon. Somebody might be curious enough to follow us."

"Have you seen anyone?"

"Well . . ."

"Who? What do they look like?"

"Mexicans. Two of them. I only got a glimpse, but they're behind us somewhere."

She shot a fearful glance at their backtrail. "I'm glad I brought a rifle. You're a better shot than I am. Maybe you should carry it."

They rode on, climbing, Ace carrying the rifle, a Whitney .45 caliber. Taking a look at their backtrail now and then, he saw no one, but he knew their trail was easy to follow.

They camped on the Rio Chiquito. Again, she quickly discouraged any romantic notions he might have had and slept far away from him. If he'd been clean and halfway decent-looking, he might have tried to get into her blankets, but as he was, he could barely stand himself.

The dun horse was leg weary, and Ace was feeling sorry for him when they climbed the last hill, rode down through some tall timber, and saw the remains of Tate's cabin.

"Is that it, Ace?"

"That's her."

"I don't see anyone. Let's hurry. I want to count that money before it gets dark."

For a moment, after Ace had carefully lifted the rat's nest and removed the floorboards, she could only gasp. "O-o-oh. My God, oh God." She picked up a double handful of coins, let them trickle through her fingers. "My God, my God."

While she was doing that, Ace went outside and studied their trail. His eyes took in every tree, boulder, and ravine. He was uneasy.

"Let's count it," she said behind him. "I never saw so much money."

"You go ahead," he said. "Put it in those saddlebags. I'll hobble the horses and keep watch."

"You think someone followed us, don't you?"

"I . . . uh . . . I don't know. What I do know is if somebody wanted to follow us, there was no way we could have hidden our trail."

"They could come up on us any time, then, couldn't they?"

"Yeah."

"What should we do?"

"Nothing now. Go ahead and count the money and fill the saddlebags."

It turned dark before she could finish. The horses were

grazing. Everything looked peaceful. The saddlebags were so heavy she had to strain to carry them outside. "I counted over fifteen hundred coins, all double eagles. That's over thirty thousand dollars, and there must be a hundred left in there. I'll have to wait 'til daylight to find them all."

"All right. We're gonna have a hard night, Marybelle."

"Why?"

"It's just a hunch. I don't know why, but I'd feel better if we don't have a fire. Or . . . maybe we ought to build a fire but stay away from it."

"Oh . . . I . . . you may be right."

They built a big fire, ate hastily from tin cans, then when it was dark, they carried a blanket apiece and the saddlebags uphill from the cabin, under the trees. From where they sat in the dark they could watch the fire slowly burn itself out.

He whispered, "Go ahead and try to sleep. I'll keep watch."

"Wake me up in a few hours, will you? Sooner if you see anything."

"Sure."

He knew from the way she kept changing positions that she was uncomfortable on the ground, but eventually she was quiet. Ace was barely able to stay awake. The quarter moon gave forth enough light for him to make out the cabin downhill from them, out in the open. But it was only a vague shape in the dark.

His head was heavy and he was blinking to keep his eyes open, when suddenly he snapped awake. Something moved down there.

Horses? No, a man. It was only a shadow, but it was shaped like a man. Eyes straining, Ace watched. Now there were two shadows that hadn't been there before. And they were moving.

He'd learned back in his coon hunting years that it

202

was better not to look directly at something you wanted to see in the dark. He concentrated on looking to the east of the shadows. Yep, they were moving, and they were too small to be horses.

As Ace watched the two shadows came together for a moment, right where the fire had been, then they moved apart and disappeared, then a few minutes later they came together again. Now a dim light flared inside the cabin. It quickly died and another light flared. A man was striking matches, trying to see what there was to see inside the cabin. A dozen matches were lighted. The shadows came back outside, so close together they looked like one. They separated, disappearing in the direction of the corral and lean-to.

Ace sat back, leaning against a tree with the rifle across his lap. No use shooting in the dark. Wait for daylight.

That's when the shooting would begin.

Twenty-eight

They were in a jackpot for sure. Two men were also waiting for daylight, knowing Ace and Marybelle would have to leave their cover among the trees and go down to the cabin to pick up the rest of the money and saddle their horses. When they did, they would be good targets. Two shots from ambush, and two killers would be rich.

Ace Bailey mulled it over and finally decided there was only one way to do it. Good thing Marybelle Stewart had ridden the outlaw trail as a youngster and knew how to use a gun. Good thing gunfire and danger were nothing new to her.

Once he had it figured out, Ace slept.

He was shivering with the dawn cold when he awakened. Stars were still visible in the sky, and the quarter moon had worked its way over to the western horizon. But the cabin could now be seen. The two horses had crow-hopped their way about two hundred yards east of the cabin and were grazing peacefully. Their saddles lay near the cabin door. It was still dark among the trees.

Ace moved only his eyes and hoped the woman would stay still. He wanted to see the two men before they saw him, see where they were. When the woman moaned and stirred, he said, "Shhh. Don't move."

Marybelle Stewart didn't move but said, in a muffled voice, "What's wrong. Is someone down there?"

"They're not far away. Two, I think. They're just waiting for us to show ourselves."

"O-o-oh. What shall we do?"

"Nothing right now. Wait and watch. Don't move any more than you have to."

"O-o-h, every bone in my body aches."

"That thirty thousand dollars ought to make you feel better."

"It won't do us any good if we're shot by robbers."

"Shhh." Ace had seen movement. He watched.

Gradually, the sky turned lighter. Now everything was visible. They were back in the trees, too, over west of the cabin by the creek, near Old Tate's grave. They didn't move much, but they moved.

Ace asked, "Can you shoot this rifle, Marybelle?"

"Yes. It's been a long time, but I can shoot."

"Here's what we'll have to do. They're over there beyond the corral, within rifle shot of the cabin. The horses are over east out of their range. I can stay in the timber where they can't get a good shot at me, cross the vega near the horses, and come up in the timber on the other side of the vega. Then I can get in the back side of the cabin."

Her eyes studied his face. "What I have to do then is keep them from going any closer, make them stay away from the cabin."

A small grin turned up one corner of his mouth. "Correct. Go to the head of the class."

"They won't get any closer, not if this rifle shoots and I'm alive."

"Atta girl. I'll snatch the saddles and get back in the timber behind the cabin and get to the horses."

"If you can do that, which way will we go? Back where we came from?"

"No. These saddlebags are heavy. We'd best take the easiest trail. That one down there prob'ly goes to Angel or Eagle Nest. We can go on down to Cimarron from there. That's downhill and not so hard on the horses.

205

They were silent a moment, then Ace said, "There. See 'em? Don't move, but look over there beyond the corral."

"Yes, I see them. They look like Mexicans. They're just waiting for us, aren't they?"

"Yeah. When they see me come out of the woods down there, they might think that's where you are. Don't let them see you, but shoot if one of them aims a rifle."

Standing slowly, Ace said, "Get behind this tree, Marybelle, on your belly."

"Ace . . . it's . . . you're . . . good luck."

He moved as cautiously as he could, keeping big ponderosas between him and the two men. When he was two hundred yards east of where he'd spent the night, Ace walked out of the woods.

He stepped lively but didn't run as he crossed the narrow valley and got into the brush along the creek. No shots had been fired yet. Keeping the cabin between him and the men, he approached it from the collapsed back side and went in. There were gold coins scattered near the spot where they'd been found. He had nothing to carry them in and had to leave them.

For a moment he'd have to expose himself to rifle fire, but it was that or ride bareback.

There was only one way to do it. Bailey stood inside and fixed the saddles in his vision, then ran. As fast as he could move, he tucked a saddle blanket under each arm, hung the bridles over the saddle horns, and grabbed a saddle in each hand.

A rifle cracked in the woods. A split second later a bullet pinged off the ground six yards from his feet. Marybelle had spoiled somebody's aim. Her rifle cracked again. By then Bailey had his hands shoved through the fork of each saddle and was backing through the door. Another rifle bullet hit the front wall of the cabin. It was a hasty shot. Again Marybelle fired. She was keeping

206

them back among the trees, not giving them a chance to take aim but giving him a chance to get into the brush again.

Bailey splashed across the creek and ran awkwardly, carrying the two saddles. They weighed about thirty-five pounds each, and he had the two saddle blankets under his arms. He ran, stumbled, and ran until he was winded. Ran until he was out of their rifle range.

More gunfire. He guessed they were returning Marybelle's fire, and he hoped she would keep her cover.

When he was opposite the horses, he ran out of the woods right at them. To the horses he looked like some strange animal, carrying the saddles, running toward them. They tried to stampede, but the hobbles kept them from going far.

"Whoa, boys. Whoa now." Bailey dropped the saddles and walked up to them, carrying bridles. More rifle fire came from the woods to the west of the cabin, but the bullets fell short. Within minutes Bailey had the two horses saddled. He swung into the saddle of the dun, grabbed the reins of Marybelle's horse, and rode at a gallop into the timber.

She was where he'd left her, on her belly, only her head and right shoulder and arm exposed to the men over west. She heard Ace coming and stood, keeping behind the tree.

"I think they're coming this way," she said. "They're trying to keep us from getting on the horses."

Dismounting, Ace said, "Give me the rifle, Marybelle, and get on your horse." She did as directed. He hung the heavy saddlebags over the saddle horns. "All right, now lead my horse. Go east. Wait for me over there somewhere."

Without a word, she mounted her horse, gave Ace a look that was half sorrow and half pleading, then socked boot heels to her horse and was riding.

They'd be coming. They'd heard her leave. He only hoped she would stay out of their sight and they would think he was with her.

Now he heard them coming. They were horseback, coming at a gallop. They were fools.

When they were close enough, Ace stepped from behind the ponderosa, rifle at his shoulder. The man in the lead was carrying a rifle in his right hand. Both reined up abruptly, surprise on their faces. Ace shot the first man through the heart. The second man threw up his left hand, trying to control his horse with his right one.

"Don't shoot. For God's sake, don't shoot."

Keeping the man's chest in the rifle sights, Ace said, "Well, I'll be damned."

The two wore Mexican sombreros on their heads and colorful serapes around their shoulders, but they were Anglos. "I've seen you before," Ace said. "In The Red Rose, back in Santa Fe."

With the fear of death written on his face, the man said, "We didn't mean you no harm. We only . . . uh . . ."

"Sure, sure." The rifle barked again.

No hurry now. Leaving the dead men where they'd fallen, Ace mounted one horse and picked up the reins of the other. A quarter of a mile ahead, he began calling, "Marybelle. Hey, Marybelle." He found her on the edge of the woods, sitting her horse, waiting.

She asked, "Is it . . . I heard two shots. Did you? . . ."

"Yeah. Let's go back and get the rest of the money."

"Were they Mexicans?"

"Naw. Damned gringos trying to look like Mexicans. One of them saw me buy a drink in The Red Rose with a double eagle, figured I had some more somewhere, and got a pal to help track us and see what we had."

"They certainly had murder on their minds, didn't they? And they figured that if they were seen, whoever

208

saw them would blame some Mexicans."

"If we'd stayed with our campfire last night, we'd be dead and they'd be rich."

While she counted and picked up the rest of the coins, he carried the two bodies on their own horses and laid them on top of Tate's grave. Ace muttered, "You were all thieves. You can keep each other company." He unsaddled their two horses and turned them loose.

At Eagle Nest, she went alone into a general store and bought a slab of bacon, a loaf of bread, and a heavy canvas bag. "We're prospecting not far from here," Marybelle said, and that was the only explanation she gave. Out of sight of the wagon road, they divided the money.

"Half is yours," she said.

"A third. That's what we agreed to."

"You've earned half. In fact, you could have kept the whole caboodle for yourself."

"If I hadn't met you, I wouldn't have known about it."

"All right, there's thirty-one thousand six hundred dollars here. You take eleven thousand and six hundred. That will leave me enough to go into business for myself."

"Fair enough."

As they rode downhill, into Cimarron Canyon, she made plans. "I can sell this horse in Cimarron and take a stage to Raton. From there, I can travel by rail to Santa Fe or wherever I want to go."

"Think you'll have any trouble spending all these double eagles?"

"No. I'm acquainted with people who can convert them to greenbacks with no trouble at all."

Grinning, he said, "It pays to know the right people."

After a moment of silence, he said, "I'll spend a night with my sister and her husband. I reckon we'd better split up before we get to town."

She shook her head. "No. We'll be seen together, but I

can say I didn't know who you are. We met on the trail and traveled together. There's no crime they can charge me with. I've stayed in the hotel before, you know, and I'll stay there until I can catch a stage."

"Maybe you're right. You'll need some help packing those saddlebags."

"There will be some very curious people, but I've got a .32 Colt in my pocket and I can take care of myself."

Ace grinned. "I don't doubt that for a second."

Twenty-nine

Cousin Jack didn't recognize Ace in the dim light from the open door, not until Ace said, "Howdy Jack."

"Damn, man, it's Alvin." He turned half around. "Mindy, me darlin', look who's out here."

Then Mindy was in the doorway, looking as if her stomach were about to pop but smiling. "Alvin. How wonderful. Get down and come in. Jack, take care of Alvin's horse."

He no more than got seated at the kitchen table when she said, "It's all over about what you did at Stockwell. It's in the *Raton Range* and people are talking about it."

"Do they know you're my sister?"

"Nobody's mentioned it. I don't think anybody around here knows. The paper says Sheriff Petersen and his deputies were rustling cattle, and it says Pop is at home recuperating from being fed too little in jail."

"Well," Ace hefted the canvas bag onto the table top, "I've got more news."

Jack came in, grinning. "Alvin, old son, nobody knows it but I'm married to the sister of a famous bad man. Damn, but you don't look like a bad man."

"He's not bad," Mindy put in. "He's just . . . well, he sure straightened out that mess in Stockwell and got Pop out of jail."

"That bloomin' sheriff got what he deserved. Darlin', put another plate on the table."

Not until he'd taken two sips of hot coffee and leaned

back in his chair did Ace say, "Mindy, take a look in that sack."

"Why, Alvin, what's? . . ." Her nimble fingers soon had the canvas bag open. "O-o-o-h, my goodness. Is it real? It can't be real. Jack, look at this."

Cousin Jack couldn't believe it. He picked out a coin, rubbed it on his shirtsleeve, bit it, rubbed it again. He looked at Ace with a question on his face.

Ace said, "I came by it honestly. I didn't steal it. It was buried up there near Eagle Nest Lake for six years. A woman I know was looking for it, and I helped her find it. This is my share."

"Damn, man."

When they finished a meal of roast beef, freshly baked bread, beans, and potatoes, Ace told them of his plans. "I can't stay in one place too long. Somebody'll get suspicious. I think I'll go down to a place called Arroyo Hondo and look for a horse I traded off a while back. If I can find him and if he's still sound and healthy, I'll buy him back and head west. I hear Phoenix is a good town, with a racetrack and a lot of running horses. That horse—Booger Bay is his name—can win a lot of short races."

"That's a long ways from home, Alvin. We won't see you again for a long time."

Ace shook his head sadly. Cousin Jack tamped rough-cut tobacco into his long-stemmed pipe, and he struck a wooden match on a suspender button. Then Ace said, "I regret that. But some day I'll be forgotten and maybe I can come back."

Jack puffed on his pipe and said, "You're bally famous. You won't be forgotten for a bloomin' long time."

Tears were running down Mindy's face now. "We won't know what became of you."

"Yeah," Ace said. He was feeling depressed.

Slowly, Mindy stood, pushing her swollen stomach

ahead of her. She put a pot of water on the stove to heat and began scraping and stacking the dishes on a table. She sniffed back tears.

"Mindy," Ace said solemnly, "sit down, will you. I want to tell you something."

She sat, still sniffling.

"There's eleven thousand six hundred dollars in that sack. I'll keep about a thousand, and I want you and Jack to keep a thousand and take the rest to Mom and Pop. Will you do that?" He looked from his sister to Cousin Jack.

"Damn, man, you don't need to give us any money."

"I want to. You're a good provider, Jack, but I want my sister—and you—to have some of the things that a working man can't buy. Will you do that?"

"We'll take the money to your folks. As soon after the baby is born that Mindy can travel, we'll go visit 'em and give 'em the money."

"You're a good man, Jack."

Mindy managed a weak smile. "Won't Mom and Pop be glad to see their grandchild. Oh, won't that make them happy."

At breakfast, after a night on the floor, Ace tried to make light of everything. "Say, tell me something, Jack. I can't figure it out. Is *bally* good or bad?"

"It's whatever you want it to be, old son. It ain't cussin', which your sister don't allow."

"Well, tell me this. Which is worse, *bally* or *bloomin'*?"

Chuckling, Jack answered, "When you hear me use them words, you'll know what I mean."

"Yeah," Ace chuckled with him. "I always know what you mean. But answer me another question. Why do some folks call you Cousin Jack? Have you got that many kin around here?"

"Naw, I ain't got no kin here, but back in King George's country, most ever'body is a kin and ever'body calls ever'body cousin. Some a' these lumberjacks have worked with the Cornish before."

Mindy said, "He came from Cornwall, England, Alvin. That's why he talks different."

"Sure, by way of Durbin and the bloomin' Kimberly mines."

Shaking his head with a grin, Bailey said, "You've got some stories to tell. Wish I could stick around to hear them."

When Jack went to work, carrying his lunch in an empty lard can, Ace asked him to keep his ears open for word about a woman alone who had a horse to sell and wanted to get to Raton. "She's the woman I told you about," he said.

Then Ace used Cousin Jack's razor to shave. Mindy gave him a haircut. He carried a washtub of warm water into the bedroom, shut the door, and took a bath while his sister washed his clothes and hung them over the stove to dry.

When he came home from the sawmill, Jack told them all about the mysterious woman. "Yep, she rode up last night, carryin' two heavy saddlebags. First thing this mornin', she sold the horse and saddle to bally ol' Charlie Hall, and of course he took unfair advantage of her like all the bloomin' horse traders do, but she was in a hurry to catch the stage to Raton."

"She got on the stage, then?"

"Yep. Wouldn't answer any questions about herself. But she'd been here before, and ever'body knew she wouldn't tell 'em a bloomin' thing."

Ace had to chuckle. "She's been on the wrong side of the law herself, but she's a good woman. I'd trust her with anything."

He was in a good mood when he rode north early in the morning. He was well fed and well rested, and so was the dun horse. He was clean, his clothes were clean, and he had a thousand dollars in double eagles in a canvas bag wrapped around his saddle horn.

Equally as important, he'd spent a night in Santa Fe without being recognized and he'd spent two nights in Cimarron without anyone asking questions. Chances were good that he could stay in Taos until he'd located and bought Booger Bay. By the time anyone knew he was here he'd be gone.

Phoenix probably wasn't as lively as El Paso, but it would do. As long as there were men who liked to bet on running horses, play cards, or gamble at just about anything else, he could make a living. He'd done it before. His folks he'd miss for sure. And Mindy. And her baby. But they'd have plenty of money and they'd be comfortable. That was something they'd never had before, and it made him happy to think about it.

Ace Bailey whistled a little tune as he rode into the Cimarron Canyon. He stayed on the road where traveling was easy and didn't try to avoid meeting anyone. He was alive, he was free, and he had money.

When rain came to the Taos Valley, it was usually short and noisy, with spectacular fireworks in the sky. But this one had turned into a steady drizzle. For two days it had drizzled, which pleased the ranchers and farmers, even though they had to put pots and buckets everywhere inside their houses to catch leaks from the roofs.

Taosenos had built most of their homes with adobe brick, and even the flat roofs were of hard-packed adobe clay. Two days of rain had turned most of them to mud. Ace Bailey had ridden into the rain twenty miles north of town, and by the time he reached the outskirts he was soaked and cold. Water dripped from his hat brim down his back. He found a place to pen and feed his horse two blocks north of the plaza, then he walked, carrying the canvas bag, to a one-story hotel on the edge of the plaza.

215

Sure enough, the roof over his room was leaking, and when he complained about it the proprietor brought him a tin bucket to catch the water. Oh well, at least the bed was dry. For the time being, anyway.

He made sure the room had a good lock, then went looking for a haberdashery to buy some dry clothes. The village had been built around the plaza, with short, crooked streets running in all directions from it, and the merchants had located their businesses within view of it. Ace made a mental note of the sheriff's office on the west side, but he wasn't worried. He'd never been in Taos before, and he wasn't known here.

An hour later he was dressed in new dry clothes and was eating a meal in El Ternero Cafe. If the Mexicans would back off a little with their hot peppers, they'd be the best cooks in the world, he thought. The steak was good, and the beans were cooked as only the Mexicans could cook them.

"Gracias, senor," the woman said when he paid with silver coins.

Outside, he turned up the collar of his new duck jacket and started across the plaza to the hotel. A man's voice behind him caused Ace to stop and look back.

"Senor, un momento, por favor."

The man was fat, with a round, smooth-shaven face, a big-brimmed hat, and a long-barreled pistol in a holster on his left hip. He also had a silver star pinned to his shirt pocket. Bailey faced him. "Yeah?"

"Senor, please to oblige me. *Por favor.* Your name, please." He was smiling a nervous smile.

Aw, damnit. What had made him suspicious? Was his picture being circulated all over the territory? Or had somebody from Arroyo Hondo recognized him and hot-footed it over to the sheriff? Damnit.

With a resigned shrug, Bailey answered, "My name is Alvin Charles Bailey."

216

The sheriff was still smiling his nervous smile. *"Senor* Bailey, I am Sheriff Roberto Gomez. Please to oblige me. I have a warrant for your arrest."

The two men faced each other in the drizzle. They were alone in the plaza.

"You know who I am?" Bailey asked.

"Yes, my fran, I know who you are. Please to hand me your *pistola* and come with me."

"Do you think you can arrest me?"

"Please, Meester Bailey. I would be obliged. My wife and my children would thank you, *tambien.*"

"Aw, for . . ." It would be easy. There wasn't another lawman in sight, and that long-barreled pistol couldn't be drawn in a hurry. One fast shot from the .38, and Bailey could walk away. Sheriff Gomez would be just one more. He'd be number . . .

Oh, Lord. He'd lost count. He didn't know how many men he'd killed.

"Please, *senor.*" The smile was gone. The nervousness remained. Sheriff Gomez was scared.

"You know what will happen if you try to draw that shooting iron."

"Si, Meester Bailey. But I have a duty."

"What will you do if I hand you my gun?"

"It is my duty, *senor*, to lock you in the jail. You will have a fair trial."

That tingle was working its way up to Bailey's chest. He stood spraddle-legged, ready. Sheriff Gomez made no threatening move. His lower lip trembled, and his normally dark face was white with fear.

And then Bailey shrugged again and relaxed. He'd broken out of jail before. He could do it again.

"All right, Mr. Gomez. I'll hand you my gun with my left hand. But whatever you do, don't draw that cannon of yours, will you."

Relief flooded the Mexican sheriff's face. *"Si, senor.*

My fran. I am obliged."

With his left hand, Bailey lifted the .38 from its holster and handed it to the sheriff. He asked, "Which way, my fran?"

Thirty

The jail was in the back half of the sheriff's office. The walls were thick adobe and the iron bars in the narrow window were deeply embedded in the walls. There were two iron cots. And there was another inmate, an Indian.

Instead of sitting on a bunk, the Indian squatted in a corner, wrapped in a blanket. His black eyes watched Bailey, but he said nothing. "How-do," Bailey said. When he got no answer, he decided there was no use trying to make conversation. Outside, it was turning dark. Bailey lay back on one of the cots, then had to move to the other. A leak had sprung in the adobe ceiling and one cot was wet.

Not long after dark, the sheriff placed a lamp on the floor in front of the cell door and said, "I'll lock the door so no one can get in, and I'll fetch *almuerzo,* your breakfast, *manana.*"

He left. The lamp put out only a dim light. The Indian didn't move from his corner. The roof leaked.

Bailey lay back on the dry bunk with his hands under his head and relaxed. A trial, the sheriff had said. He'd been through a trial before and was yet to be convicted. A warrant? The only disagreement he'd had in this county was over a horse trade at Arroyo Hondo. And the other man had had a gun pointed at him. There were witnesses. Maybe not to the shooting, but townsmen had seen the dead cowboy's body with a gun in its hand. The gun had been fired. Self-defense was a good defense in a trial.

The leak in the ceiling was getting worse. Now it was

leaking over both cots. Bailey had to move.

Squatting on the floor, across the room from the toilet bucket, Bailey watched mud fall from the ceiling. If this kept up, the whole damned cell would be flooded before morning. More mud fell.

"Goddamn." Bailey looked over at the Indian. If the Indian had seen anything, his face didn't register it. His face just didn't register. "It's getting wet in here," Bailey said. Still no change of expression. "Oh well, maybe you don't savvy English."

Now a section of the roof fell in, missing Bailey by only a foot. Looking up, he could see the sky. The drizzling rain was coming through a hole in the ceiling. "Goddamn."

The Indian stood and dropped the blanket. He was short, potbellied, and dressed in a white man's dirty cotton shirt and pants, but with moccasins on his feet. He dragged one of the cots under the hole in the ceiling.

Bailey said, "You're not . . . well, by God, I believe you are."

The Indian reached up and got his hands outside on the edge of the hole. With the strength in his arms he pulled himself up, getting his head outside, then his shoulders. A few wiggles and kicks, and he was gone.

As he disappeared, more of the ceiling caved in.

"Well, I'll be goddamned," Bailey said.

He, too, stood on the cot, reached up, and got hold of the edge of the cavity. Straining, grunting, he pulled himself up, not as easily as the Indian had, but he got himself out onto the roof just the same.

Now the roof was caving in so fast that Bailey was afraid to stand, to put all his weight on one spot. He began crawling on his belly to the nearest wall. The rain came down.

Then the roof gave way under him and he fell back inside the jail.

Headfirst.

Thirty-one

The only undertaker in the Taos Valley made a small fortune on the way to Stockwell. In his mind he'd earned it. He had the body laid out in new clothes, polished boots pointed up, the hands crossed at the belt, the blond hair combed, and the eyes closed. He even had the pearl-handled silver-plated Colt in its holster at the right side.

The news had spread. All along the route people were more than willing to pay a quarter each to see the body. He took the long route in his black hearse with glass sides, drawn by two black horses. He stopped at Espanola, Santa Fe, Las Vegas, Springer, and Raton. Luck was with him. The sky stayed cloudy and the weather cool. Every time he opened the lid of the muslin-lined wooden casket, people gasped, oohed and aahed. Some murmured prayers, and always at least one young woman whispered, "Oh, ain't he handsome."

At Cimarron, Mrs. Jack Wembley couldn't stop crying until her son was born, then her motherly instincts took over and all her attention was given to the baby. She named him Alvin Charles Wembley, and she was so proud she couldn't stop smiling.

By the time the undertaker got back to Taos, Sheriff Gomez had announced that he would not be a candidate for reelection. He was lucky to be alive and he knew it. He thanked the Virgin Mary every day, and he made sure the thousand dollars in gold coins found in Ace Bailey's hotel room was handed over to the next of kin — after the undertaker deducted his fee, of course. And while he was praying, he asked that people forget he was the sheriff who had arrested Ace Bailey.

Alvin Charles Bailey was buried in a small cemetery at Stockwell. Everyone in Stockwell County came for the funeral. Not long after that, the Reverend and Mrs. Bailey sold their farm and moved to town. They no longer had to hoe weeds, cut and bundle the maize, shuck the corn, and pray for enough summer rain. The reverend spent most of his time writing his sermons.

In Albuquerque, citizens watched a new brick building go up. They were told it was going to be the finest pleasure emporium this side of St. Louis, better even than The Red Rose in Santa Fe. When the doors to The Marybelle Palace finally opened, a smiling Marybelle Stewart herself was on hand to greet everyone.

Yes, she said, she had been with Ace Bailey for many days and nights when he was outfoxing the officers of the law. That Whitney rifle on display above the bar was the one he had used to kill two men who intended to kill and rob them. And, she admitted boldly, she was the one who had slipped him a gun and helped him escape from the Stockwell County jail. When anyone had nerve enough to ask where she got the money to build The Palace, she only smiled and mentioned Ace Bailey. Some folks were convinced she had helped him pull off a robbery somewhere, but no lawman could find a robbery in which he was a suspect.

Back in Stockwell, the tombstone over Ace Bailey's grave read simply:

Alvin Charles Bailey
1865-1886
R.I.P.

On a moonless night it disappeared. County residents figured the thieves hoped to sell it as a souvenir. Officers of the law all over the Southwest were on the lookout. But the thieves apparently decided it was dangerous to be seen with the tombstone, and they hid it.

One day it will be found.

222

POWELL'S ARMY
BY TERENCE DUNCAN

#1: UNCHAINED LIGHTNING   (1994, $2.50)

Thundering out of the past, a trio of deadly enforcers dispenses its own brand of frontier justice throughout the untamed American West! Two men and one woman, they are the U.S. Army's most lethal secret weapon—they are POWELL'S ARMY!

#2: APACHE RAIDERS   (2073, $2.50)

The disappearance of seventeen Apache maidens brings tribal unrest to the violent breaking point. To prevent an explosion of bloodshed, Powell's Army races through a nightmare world south of the border—and into the deadly clutches of a vicious band of Mexican flesh merchants!

#3: MUSTANG WARRIORS   (2171, $2.50)

Someone is selling cavalry guns and horses to the Comanche—and that spells trouble for the bluecoats' campaign against Chief Quanah Parker's bloodthirsty Kwahadi warriors. But Powell's Army are no strangers to trouble. When the showdown comes, they'll be ready—and someone is going to die!

#4: ROBBERS ROOST   (2285, $2.50)

After hijacking an army payroll wagon and killing the troopers riding guard, Three-Fingered Jack and his gang high-tail it into Virginia City to spend their ill-gotten gains. But Powell's Army plans to apprehend the murderous hardcases before the local vigilantes do—to make sure that Jack and his slimy band stretch hemp the legal way!